# Walter Plume and the Dehydrated Imagination

Rebecca Lynn Morales

# Walter Plume and the Dehydrated Imagination

SWEETWATER
BOOKS
AN IMPRINT OF CEDAR FORT, INC.
SPRINGVILLE, UTAH

ISBN 13: 978-1-4621-1780-2

Published by Sweetwater Books, an imprint of Cedar Fort, Inc.
2373 W. 700 S., Springville, UT 84663
Distributed by Cedar Fort, Inc., www.cedarfort.com

LIBRARY OF CONGRESS CATALOGING-IN-PUBLICATION DATA
Names: Morales, Rebecca Lynn, author.
Title: Walter Plume and the dehydrated imagination / Rebecca Lynn Morales.
Description: Springville, Utah : Sweetwater Books, an imprint of Cedar Fort, Inc., [2016] | ©2016 | Summary: Waiting in Aunt Cecilia's truck while she sells hand-carved statues door-to-door makes Walter Reed feel as if his imagination is starving to death -- until he steps outside and discovers that bright green grass sprouts beneath his feet.
Identifiers: LCCN 2015032101 | ISBN 9781462117802 (pbk. : alk. paper)
Subjects: | CYAC: Gardens--Fiction. | Droughts--Fiction. | Magic--Fiction. | Imagination--Fiction. | Imaginary creatures--Fiction. | Good and evil--Fiction. | LCGFT: Fiction.
Classification: LCC PZ7.1.M6685 Wal 2016 | DDC [Fic]--dc23
LC record available at http://lccn.loc.gov/2015032101

Cover design by Michelle May Ledezma
Cover design © 2016 Cedar Fort, Inc.
Edited and typeset by Melissa J. Caldwell

Printed in the United States of America

10 9 8 7 6 5 4 3 2 1

Printed on acid-free paper

*To Gabriel, my husband, my love.*
*Your encouragement released my imagination*
*from the shadows.*

# Contents

## CHAPTER ONE
# Angel Victory

A garden has a life of its own; if you listen closely, you can hear a heartbeat, a rhythm. That's what my Uncle Andre would tell me. Once, I thought I heard the beat of my uncle's cottage garden. *Swoosh, hum, swoosh, hum.* But maybe it was just the washing machine.

*Thump, bump, thump, bump* was the sound of my heartbeat as we rolled along the curvy mountain road way too slow.

Uncle Andre used to drive this old blue pickup with the windows down like he was in a race to win millions of dollars. By the time we got to where we were going, Uncle Andre would say, "Boy, you look like you stuck your finger in a light socket." No matter what I was doing, my crazy hair seemed to have a mind of its own. My sixth grade school portrait resembled Einstein in all his glory. Except my mop is ashy brown, not white.

Today my aunt Cecelia was driving, and she was taking her sweet ol' time.

"I'm bored," I said.

She just stared out the windshield. I wanted to say she was looking at the road ahead of us, but I wasn't sure that was what she was seeing.

"Aunt Cecelia, can we at least turn on the radio?"

"I'm not in the mood right now, Walter," she said. Her face drooped with sadness. I knew to leave it alone.

I closed my eyes. I could feel the warmth from the sunlight as it bounced off of my glasses. Uncle Andre had dark-framed specs just like mine, and wild hair too.

*Light, dark. Light, dark. Sunlight, shadows.*

I opened my lids and gazed at the trees creeping past us. The limbs and leaves seemed to melt together into images. Pictures of things. I saw an old lady in a rocking chair, Tarzan swinging from a vine, and a dog jumping after a ball. Cool. Yes, this shadow game would keep my mind swirling until we got there.

A monkey. An alligator. A man fishing. He caught a shark. And it ate him!

*Sunlight, shadows. Sunlight, shadows.*

*HONK!*

All of a sudden, our truck swerved off the road and into the weeds and bushes along the shoulder. Aunt Cecelia struggled to gain control of the steering wheel as we bumped and turned all over the place. We lurched to a stop just before the front end of the truck collided with a boulder.

I threw my hands in the air. “What happened?”

“Oh, I’m so sorry, Walter. I must have drifted into the other lane.” Her hands were shaking and her salt and pepper bun (mostly pepper) had toppled over to one side of her head.

“Are you okay?” I asked.

“I think so. . . . Oh no!” Aunt Cecelia jerked her seat belt loose and leapt from the truck.

I pried open my door and raced to the side of the truck bed. Climbing up on the back wheel, I stood to get a good look inside of the bed. I was, after all, the shortest eleven-year-old on the planet.

Aunt Cecelia’s eyes were filled with tears. Three of her five clay sculptures were broken. Two abstract creations were broken in half. (Honestly, I couldn’t really tell what they were supposed to be.) The large owl had shattered into a million pieces. All that remained were two tall angels. One held a sword and the other a trumpet. They stood over the broken pieces like they had just won a battle.

"I can't believe this," she whispered as she began to cry. The weighty sadness hung on her face like a lure at the end of my fishing line about to sink into the dark water.

I felt I should say something, but I couldn't find any words. Not even a sound. I padded around the truck and took her hand. I just stood there and held it.

After all her tears had left her, she looked up and said, "I feel dehydrated." Then she started to laugh. I hadn't heard my aunt laugh in months. It wasn't a joyful laugh really—more of an uncontrollable giggle. It made me more nervous than the crying.

"Maybe we should just go home," I said.

"We can't, my dear. We have no choice. We need to sell the two sculptures we have left."

"What if I got a job instead?"

"Don't be silly, Walter. You're only eleven years old. You have to go to school. And I'm going to sell these sculptures to pay for it. Now, grab me my water jug."

After Aunt Cecelia took several gulps, we crawled back into the pickup and eased back onto the road.

*I could get a job*, I thought. I could mow lawns. I could craft my own fishing lures and sell them on the Internet. Or I could be a cook in a restaurant. I had learned a lot from my parents' chef, Algernon. In the evenings when they were out, he would whip me up the most delicious meals with flavors and spices most kids hated: truffle oil, liver, poached salmon. I learned to appreciate fine cuisine. (My favorite, though, was still a good ol' hot dog with ketchup and mustard.)

"I'm hungry," I moaned, just as we turned left onto a long gravel driveway.

"We're here. I think." Aunt Cecelia lowered her window. She reached out and wiped the dust from the numbers on a stone pilaster.

Before us loomed a rusted brass gate covered in dead vines and dust.

"Are you sure?" I asked.

"This is the address."

"Maybe you got it wrong. This doesn't look like an estate of any kind."

"I'm not the one who made this appointment." She swallowed hard and stared out the window again.

"Oh."

We climbed out of the truck and together pushed the right side of the gate open. I couldn't imagine such a drab place having need of or even wanting my aunt's statues. We made our way up the pebbly road lined with leafless trees.

Just over a small hill, we saw the house: "The French Chateau." It was ugly. The paint was peeling off. Cobwebs consumed the corners of every window, hazy with dust. As far as I could see, there was nothing but dirt and shriveled up, dead plants. Yup, definitely not the stately mansion my aunt had described. I'm no expert salesman, but I could tell this dump's owner wouldn't be the ideal client.

All I could think was, *Great, another dull afternoon*. Another day without the excitement and adventure Uncle Andre had laced through our special story times.

Aunt Cecelia peered at that crusty house for a long time. The ever-present sadness had settled into the bags under her blue eyes. She mulled over that shabby structure as though she had seen it before. Finally, after a deep breath, she said, "Okay, I'm going in."

"I'm going with you," I said, mostly because I was itching to take a look around. But also because I didn't want my aunt to go alone. She needed a sidekick to go into a house looking that shady.

"No, you're not. Stay in the car until I get back."

"What? I've waited this long, and I don't even get to get out?" My anger bubbles started to boil over.

"Listen, Walter, we can't afford to have this go wrong."

"Arghhhh! Why does this always happen to me?!" I kicked the glove compartment. It popped open, spilling a ton of junk onto the floor. My anger bubbles had overflowed once again.

Stone-faced, Aunt Cecelia said, "Clean that up." Then she slipped out of the truck.

She lugged those heavy angel statues, which were over half her size, to the faded turquoise door one at a time, then rang the doorbell.

After a moment, the door opened.

A crumbling fountain blocked my view of who greeted her.

I looked down and scanned the pile of papers and trinkets. Sales receipts, junk mail, used toothpicks, a key chain from the Grand Canyon . . . and a small origami lion made from shiny gold paper.

Plucking the lion out of the rubble, I examined it. The folds were crisp and the ears and paws came to sharp points, like someone had carefully folded it only seconds ago. A tab of paper poked out of the lion's mouth with an arrow pointing inward. I pulled the tab and the paper extended like a tongue. In black ink was a quote:

*A cheerful look brings joy to the heart;*
*good news makes for good health.*

Oh. Why did I have to get so mad?

I looked up just in time to see my aunt carrying the last statue into the house. I let go of the tab. It slowly retracted into the lion's mouth, as though the king of cats were lapping up water. I knew it wasn't my aunt's fault we were in this position. She was doing the best she could, but I needed to get outside, to run, to see the light. My inner pot of fury was about to erupt and blow my imagination all over everything.

Time crept by, hour after endless hour. Okay, it was probably only five minutes, but it felt like an eternity. Then came the inevitable moment when I decided to get out of the car.

I shoved the origami lion into my hoodie pocket for safekeeping and quietly pushed open the truck door.

With one eye on the chateau's front door, I inched my foot toward the dead lawn. When my canvas high-top touched the ground, I gasped and wrenched my foot back inside the truck. Did I just see that?

I lowered my foot down once again. . . .

A thick tuft of bright green grass miraculously sprouted under my shoe.

I laughed. "This is so cool."

CHAPTER TWO

# Garden Superhero

I hopped around the front yard, stepping here and then there.

*Green. Green. Green.*

Then I spotted a shriveled, sad-looking little flower. I picked up its head in my hands, and it blossomed with soft, bright red petals.

*Green. Green. Green. Red!*

The red flower was attached to a dark green stem that traveled down to wisps of grass around its base. Squatting down among the surroundings of dirt and decay, I examined the little flower, which glowed like a beacon of hope. I had brought this colorful flower back to life!

*I'm like a superhero*, I thought. Jumping up, I threw

my arms in the air and welcomed the applause of my imaginary fans. *Thank you, thank you! You're too kind!* I looked back down at the flower that had slipped from my grip, and it had returned to its original dried-out state. *Aw, man. That's weird.* It was the same with my feet too. With each step, the bright green grass would grow up around my foot, but when I lifted my foot, the grass would disappear.

The magic worked with my hands and feet. . . . *Sooo,* I wondered. I meandered over to a dried-up hedge and wriggled my bum against it. What else would a person do with a superpower such as this? A new hedge of tiny yellow-green leaves grew underneath my legs, lifting me off my feet.

"Owwww, ow, ow!" The branches grew thorns, which started poking me all over. I tumbled off the bush and crashed onto the ground face-first.

That hurt too.

I rolled over onto my back. A plush, cool bed of moss had grown beneath me.

*This is it!* I thought. This was the kind of magical place Uncle Andre had been telling me about all those summers. I remembered how I would perch myself on the porch rail with a glass of iced grape soda in my hand and listen with anticipation as Uncle Andre unraveled his grand sagas. Up until this moment, I wasn't positive whether they were real or made up. Dragons, glow-in-the-dark people, and talking plants. It certainly was fun to think about anyway.

Aunt Cecelia would interweave the names and types of various plants to make the stories more educational. I'd learned some cool things about plants over the years.

"The Tale of the Garden Maze" was one of Uncle Andre's best stories. He always began the tale the same way: "The gardens of this one particular manor were so beautiful, I thought my heart stopped beating for at least . . . ten seconds." (He had a way of being melodramatic.) "The deep green hedges formed walls so tall I could not see over the tops, even if I stood on my tiptoes." ('Course, that isn't saying much, as Uncle Andre received the community center's "Short Man of the Year" award a few years back.) In one area, he explained, the hedges formed a maze with only one way in and seemingly only one way out.

"The hedge was an Arborvitae 'Green Giant,'" Aunt Cecelia would interject. "It can grow up to fifty feet tall." Uncle Andre would wait patiently until she was finished with her facts, then continue the story.

"As the owners of the manor continued their garden tour with your aunt Cecilia, I slunk toward the maze," Uncle Andre said. Something beckoned him from behind the dark wood door that closed off the entrance. At this point, he would raise his arms and shrug. "I couldn't help it," he'd say. "I felt that itchy-itch-itching curiosity way down deep inside." Then Aunt Cecelia would always shake her head and smile.

I've had that same itch deep down inside my gut on numerous occasions. This day was one of those times.

Uncle Andre said he pulled open the maze's heavy door, which made a sharp creak. Once inside, there were only two choices of travel among the foliage. The path to the left was wide and well lit. It looked as if that was the path that most had taken, because the ground was worn and the way was clear. The path to the right was narrow with vines and branches crisscrossing the trail. He said, "It's always more fun to take the unexplored path." A small, yet glorious light appeared down the narrow path. The light danced around and radiated unending joy. He could not take his eyes off it.

Dried leaves crunched beneath his feet as Uncle Andre stepped onto the unused pathway. He pursued the light, which led him through the maze this way, then that way. The closer he got to the light, the more the vines and branches entangled around him.

At this point in the story, his voice lowered to a stage whisper as if what happened next was a deep dark secret. "Oh no, wait! My foot was caught!" he'd say with wide eyes. At first, he thought it was a root. But then he realized that whatever it was had a tight grip on his ankle and . . .

*BONK!*

"Hey!" I said, sitting up from my daydream. Something had just hit me on the right side of my forehead. "Geez, this place is dangerous."

Maybe an acorn fell or something. I looked over the ground and lying beside me was a dirty stone, one that I hadn't noticed before. Pebbles don't fall from trees. Pebbles are thrown. Chills ran over me, leaving behind trails of goose bumps. I sprung to my feet.

Spinning around, I didn't see anyone anywhere. Aunt Cecelia was still tucked away inside the creepy house.

I thought about retreating to the truck, where nothing would, as Aunt Cecilia said, go wrong. But those goose bumps had turned into an unbearable itch. I couldn't help myself. I had to scratch it, right?

I dashed in the direction from which it seemed the rock had been thrown, creating clumps of grass, shiny pebbles, and flowery ground cover beneath my feet with each stride.

I rounded the side of the house and entered the rear yard. There were rusted-out gates and a broken down bistro table.

No life in sight.

To the left was a corroded, dried-out reflection pond. Its crumbly, rectangular edge stood about eight inches above the ground. I sat atop it, making it whole with my touch. Shiny, smooth, good as new.

Hmmm.

I lowered my hand into the empty pond and palmed the dry floor. It suddenly filled with cool, clear water, which rose up and covered my hand. Sparkling turquoise and orange tiles popped out from the pond's cement walls. This was crazy!

I dipped both hands into the water, scooped some out, and gulped it up. It tasted fresh and clean as though it had bubbled up from a spring. It put bottled water to shame.

Right as I was about to gulp some more, I saw the pond had dried up. All the water had disappeared the moment I removed my hands. Why wouldn't it stay?

I placed my hand inside, filling the fountain again.

*Empty, filled. Empty, filled.*

I could see my reflection in the water. My curious hazel eyes were looking back at me.

Wait . . . What!

There beside me was a reflection of large, dark . . . lovely . . . eyes.

Those were definitely not mine. They belonged to a girl.

My heart stopped beating for at least . . . twenty seconds.

CHAPTER THREE

# Angry Elf

*Oh, great. I've been caught*, I thought. *I got out of the car and now I'm in trouble. And my heart isn't beating and I can't breathe. What's happening to me?*

"*Bienvenue.*" The lovely eyes had a lovely voice, too.

Wait, is she talking in French? "Uh?" I mumbled.

"Welcome," she said in English.

Fumbling to my feet, I turned around and responded quite articulately, "I, uh, um . . . so, uh . . ."

"You've come back!" she exclaimed with a look of longing on her pretty face.

Come back? I had no idea what she was talking about. All I could do was stand there and stare at her. She was an inch or so shorter than me with wavy black hair swooped back on each side in tiny braids, meeting in the middle. The tops of her ears came to delicate points. She looked like an elf, like someone my uncle would have described in one of his stories. Awesome! Her almond shaped eyes sparkled dark green. Like emeralds or ferns or boiled artichokes. As green as the grass protruding from beneath my feet.

Oh no! Had she noticed the grass? She definitely saw the water in the pond. I lifted one foot. If a few blades poked out from just one foot, maybe she wouldn't notice. I swayed back and forth, beads of sweat cropping up on my forehead. Then to my surprise, that sweet-looking little elf punched me in the shoulder.

"Hey," I said, rubbing my shoulder. "What was that for?"

"You seemed stunned or something. Just wanted to bring you back to reality."

"Reality? Girl, nothing about this is real," I said, firmly planting both feet.

"My name is Aimee. And it's real, all right." She scanned our surroundings with a creased brow. "We need to talk someplace secure. Follow me." Then she dashed into a small opening in the thick brush a few yards away.

A conundrum. That's what this was. A difficult puzzle. Should I trust this pale-skinned pointy-eared girl who just socked me—and who no doubt was the person who chucked a rock at my head earlier—or obey Aunt Cecelia and go back to the truck? Why was I even debating this? My legs felt as heavy as Sequoia trunks, thick and solid, their roots stretching deep into the ground. I couldn't just stand there, uncertain, and morph into the landscape.

*What would Uncle Andre do?* I thought.

Aimee poked her head out of the brush and whispered, "Come on. We're not safe here."

I ran to catch up.

If Uncle Andre were here, he would have led the way. Forging through the bushes in Aimee's wake, everything I touched or brushed up against came to life. Glimpses of vibrant colors shot up tree branches and spilled onto their leaves.

"Stop touching everything," Aimee scolded. "I'll hold the branches out of the way for you." She pushed back a brittle branch but let go too soon; the limb slapped me in the face, blossoming with lime-green leaves on contact.

"Ow!" I glared at her as clusters of strange purplish fruit popped out of the blooms. I was kinda over this girl.

"Oh, I'm sorry," she said, pulling me through the branch of fragrant fruit bulbs. As she dragged me one way and then another, I couldn't figure out what direction we would turn next. The trails seemed indefinable.

We eventually halted behind a row of ashen, sky-scraping, cylindrical cypress trees.

"We can rest here for a moment," Aimee said. "You're looking a little . . . haggard."

I leaned against a tree and tried to catch my breath. Physical fitness was not my area of expertise. I was cut from the golf team, the only sport socially acceptable to my haughty parents. Behind me, deep-green streaks propelled like lightning all the way up the thick foliage. The scale-like leaves plumped up like they had been stung by a bee.

Aimee's head snapped up. "Oh no!" She gasped, jerking me away from the tree.

"Hey, watch it!" I said, rolling my arm around a suddenly sore socket. "You're strong for a girl."

Aimee ignored me, focusing on the tree until every last leaf shriveled back into dust. She rotated around and tilted her head, angling her pointy ears. It seemed she was listening for something, anything.

Wind whistled through the lifeless landscape.

"It's going to be harder than I thought keeping you hidden," she said through a clenched jaw. "Try not to touch anything. NOTHING."

I'd had about enough of being snapped at, yanked

around, and dragged through prickly vegetation. I got out of the car for some fun, not to be bossed around every five seconds by another control freak. More anger bubbles. *Bubbling, bubbling.*

"What's your problem?" I blurted out.

"Listen, kid—" she started.

"Whoa, wait a minute. My name is Walter Plume. And you need to understand a couple of things. I've never been here before. I don't know who you are or where you're taking me. I didn't ask to be in this dried-out, old dump. So what's going on?"

Her wide eyes melted into saggy sadness.

*Not another crier*, I thought.

Then her saggy sadness pulled in to a tight grimace. I braced myself in case she took another swing at me. Through pursed lips, she somberly said, "You're not quite what I expected. I thought you'd be more . . . I don't know . . . tough, I guess. But you have the Life-power and I—we—need you, Walter. We need your help to restore imagination and bring life back to our people."

Near exasperation, she pointed to the giant cypress. "See? Ickabod Von Snot-hook is destroying Fantaisie! You're the only one who can stop him."

I was lost. "I, uh . . . huh? What's a snot-hook?"

Aimee sighed, then spoke in a pleasant tone I hadn't

heard since her "*Bienvenue.*" "Please, Walter. Just come with me to meet my father."

She was trying to be nice, but I had a feeling she would do whatever it took to get me to wherever we were going.

"Do you have any idea what it's like to be forbidden to sing? Or dance or laugh?" Desperation poured out of Aimee's mouth. "For every moment of your life to be on a rigid, unbreakable schedule?"

I knew exactly how she felt.

My parents were prickly, uptight robots. They lived in a world of standardization. Everyone should dress and speak properly—their version of proper. We had lived in a large, gray, two-story house in the middle of the city. The streets were so clean you could eat off of them, but of course, if you wanted to, that wouldn't be allowed. Summers were the worst. There was nothing to do. A kid couldn't even kick a rock down the sidewalk—if there was one to kick.

One day, when I was eight, I was strolling home from school on my usual route. I passed the post office and the nail salon on my way to the outdoor market, where I planned to grab an apple to eat or perhaps kick down the street, if I could get away with it.

Just then, I noticed a shiny rock propping up the leg of a fruit cart. Finally, something to play with! I thought. The whirlpool of my rigid, blasé existence had been sucking me under. That tiny beaming rock was my rescue.

Blinded by excitement, I yanked the rock from beneath the cart leg, unleashing an avalanche of produce. Oranges, apples, lemons, and more plummeted down the street as I fled the scene. Our hollow doorbell rang about a half hour later. It was the fuming owner of the fruit cart, come to tattle on me. I tried to explain. I had merely looked at—okay, barely touched—a desirable kicking rock. And in so doing, at no fault of my own, the cart collapsed in the downward direction of the hill.

My explanation was unacceptable and I was told to give the produce man back his rock. "I'm sorry, sir," I said. "You can't have your rock back. That rock is my salvation, and I simply won't part with it." My parents were shocked and embarrassed. Heaven forbid I keep a little ol' rock that I found fair and square. That was the first summer they sent me to stay with Uncle Andre and Aunt Cecelia.

"Walter!" Aimee was up in my face, staring at me with wrinkled brow. "Do you need some help coming back to reality again?"

"No, I don't, thank you very much. I'll meet your father," I said.

"Good. We must be careful. Ickabod cannot know you have arrived. Keep an eye out for his Stooges," Aimee warned.

"His what?" I asked.

"They look like me, except mean. You'll see. I don't have time to explain. Let's go."

We hiked across acres of parched land, through withered trees and plants. Dried leaves and debris crunched beneath Aimee's strides. But my footsteps were silent, cushioned by new growth.

*Oh, Aunt Cecelia's gonna be upset with me*, I thought, as we marched farther and farther away from the truck. I was careful not to touch too much. Along the way we passed a long rectangular swimming pool filled with dirt and sun-baked leaves instead of water. I pictured the pool filled to the brink with crystal clear water and surrounded by shimmery blades of grass with tiny pink flowers. I imagined I could cannon ball into the deep end. *Splash!* We circled halfway around a worn-out tennis court. The net lay limp on the ground in heart-broken remembrance of games once played.

*Shadow. Dark. Shadow. Dark. Only dark now . . .*

A permanent cloud cover had settled over this part of the land. I hadn't noticed it before. The air was musty, like my week-old sweaty socks at the bottom of my locker—an unforgettable odor.

Aimee, who had been quiet most of the trip, turned to me with those big eyes and said, “I need to show you something. We can see it from the outlook at the top of this path.”

We ventured up a steep spiral walkway. At the top, the outlook was lined with large, potted, leafless trees. Crouching behind a bronze pot, Aimee unraveled the tale for me.

“Walter, look at our land.” We scanned the vast view. Everything was dead except for a tiny sliver of green all the way around the horizon.

“Where is that greenery coming from way over there?” I questioned.

“Those are other regions that have not yet been overthrown by Ickabod. For this very reason he has forbidden entry into all high places to keep my people—the Fantaisies—from seeing and trying to escape into a new land. But the truth is, we know,” Aimee muttered. “We know, but we will not abandon our land. We still have memories of what this place, the Garden, used to be. We hold tightly to them, no matter how faded they become.” Her sadness had sunk into her shoulders and trickled down her arms, meeting two tight, angry fists.

“How did this happen?” I wondered aloud.

“You see that ominous stone structure on the eastern edge of Fantaisie? Inside are three fountains.

The Fountain of Moxie, the Fountain of Whimsey, and the Fountain of Topsy-Turvy. They look the same, but the water flowing from each one is wildly different. The Fantaisies were forbidden in the Ancient Book of the Laws to drink of the fountain on the left, the Fountain of Moxie.

"Why?" I asked. "Is it poisonous?"

"Not in the way you imagine," she said. I wanted a better explanation than that but she proceeded with her storytelling.

"Driven by vanity, Ickabod felt he had a right to drink from any fountain he wanted. How dare anything, especially some old book, forbid him from doing anything, he said. He scooped a handful of the fountain's water and slurped it down. And when he did, he felt a sense of . . . control."

That word made Aimee shudder, and as she rubbed her goose-bumped arms, she looked both ways like she was about to cross a street and then scurried behind a much larger planted pot. I hurried after her, still not sure exactly what we were hiding from.

Shielded by the pot, she dished out more of the story.

"Enjoying his newfound power, he drank and then drank some more. He felt as if he could control anything and everything, and he went about doing so.

He brainwashed an army of Stooges and took over the whole land. Each time he took a drink from the fountain, trees would shrivel up into brown skeletons or an acre of grass would go crunchy. And every time he felt someone was outshining him, he would take another drink to feel in control. Over time, the entire land became completely dried out—dehydrated."

Suddenly, I felt really thirsty. I, too, knew the frustrations and emptiness of a blah life. Our eyes locked in a moment of understanding. *You have bursting anger bubbles too*, I thought. Hence the punching. "What exactly does this have to do with me?" I asked.

"Everything," said a deep, strained voice from behind us.

*Stooges!* I thought. I leapt to my feet and spun around. What? We were blocked in by a crowd of pointy ears and probing eyes. Where had they all come from?

## CHAPTER FOUR
# Roots and Flowers

Dozens of elves crouched behind us, dressed in grunge hipster attire. I hadn't really noticed Aimee's tweed vest and lace-up boots, until now. They dressed cool. A little drab, but cool. They appeared to be harmless, except for their speculative, squinting eyes.

"Walter, these are my people, the Fantaisie people of the Garden," Aimee said. Kneeling next to a moistureless hawthorn bush, she spoke to a gray-bearded elf.

"*Pourquoi étes-vous venus*? What are you doing here? Ickabod's Stooges could discover us here." The old, worn out man held up a tiny pink flower.

Aimee gasped. "Where did you find that?" Her horrified expression made me self-conscious. That pink flower looked exactly like the ones I imagined near the swimming pool. My cheeks grew warm with the unveiling of my superhero power.

Then an incredibly short Fantaisie, even stumpier than me, emerged from the crowd. "Our scouts found this flower by the swimming pool."

Yup, that was my handiwork.

"We knew that our guest had arrived," he said.

I opened my mouth to protest being their guest but only quiet came out. The clean, bright circle of concrete, with mint green baby's breath flowers beneath my feet said enough.

Aimee took the flower from the elderly man. Twirling the stem between her fingers she said, "But that doesn't make any sense. The color and life doesn't linger after he's lifted his touch. The new life only stays with him."

*That's right. But that's the flower in my imagination. Strange.*

The grizzled old man coughed, and a gray hue crept across his bony face. Aimee rushed to his side, wrapping her hands around his.

"Walter, this is my father, Pierre-Louis. He's the leader of our people. He has been ill for many months. Nothing we've tried makes him better. He's lost his hope, Walter." Tears simmered in her eyes. "Father, you should have stayed in bed."

In his weakness, the tired, vintage soul spoke with shaky voice, "We have been waiting for you, Walter."

"What do you mean, 'waiting for me'?" I asked.

"You are the one who has been sent to restore the dreams of this land, to restore the beauty and power of imagination back to the people," he said.

"Uhh . . . I beg your pardon?" High expectations made me anxious.

"You have been here before, and we have been waiting for your return."

"Uh, no. No. Like I told Aimee, I've never been here before. I've never restored anything." I started to inch backward, away from the Fantaisies, away from their pleas for salvation.

Over the last three years, I desperately desired to go on an adventure with Uncle Andre. Just like the one I was somehow in right now, but panic was sweeping over me. I had wanted to go with Uncle Andre, but he wasn't here. I didn't want to do this alone.

*Why do they recognize me? Uncle Andre . . .* My embittered grief was climbing up from deep within its hideaway, the pit of my stomach.

I reached into my hoodie pockets and crossed my arms over my belly in a hug only to brush my fingers up against the paper lion. Then I remembered the words of the lion. "A cheerful look brings joy to the heart; good news makes for good health."

"You can trust us, Walter," Aimee pleaded. "We know you have the power to save us. The Ancient Book of the Laws tells us that the one who creates life can restore all that is lost. Grass grows beneath your feet! Your imaginative mind has not been infiltrated by the tiresome, mind-numbing rules of Ickabod Von Snothook." She was smiling, almost.

Pierre-Louis swayed side to side like he was seasick and about to throw up. He looked like he could use some good news. Up until this point I had never been anybody's good news. Except maybe for Uncle Andre and Aunt Cecelia. And I wanted to bring some joy and good health to these people.

Smiling awkwardly, I said, "I'll help you. I'm not sure how, but I'd like to try."

Aimee leaped up and hugged me tight. "Thank you!"

"Uh . . . what, where . . . uh, yeah. . . ." I was quite articulate once again.

The vertically challenged Fantaisie stepped up and said, "I'm Troy. We must get you to Crinkle. We have a little less than an hour left."

"An hour left before what?" I asked. "And who's Crinkle?" This was all happening so fast.

"He's my brother," Aimee said. "And every day at two o'clock sharp, we have inspection in the main courtyard. If anyone's missing, the Stooges will track us down and make us sit in a square room with gray walls and eat plain potatoes with no spice for three days. . . . No spice, Walter!"

I was beginning to understand the depth of their situation.

The Fantaisies quickly and quietly dispersed in all directions. Troy surveyed the surroundings before rolling back a rough, irregular stone, revealing a passageway into the side of a hill. For a small dude, he sure was strong.

We hurried down into the underground passage, weeds and roots popping up like kernels in a skillet. Dim lanterns hung on the walls several yards apart, leaving some dark stretches. We started running around bends and kinks, the tunnel getting skinnier and skinnier.

Before I realized, my shoulders and legs brushed up against the sides of the tunnel and I was stuck, entwined in a curtain of vines and roots. Troy, right on my tail, slammed into the offshoots.

"What in the world?" he gasped.

"Um, help," I said.

"What'd you do?" he asked.

"Apparently, I touched something." *Geez, why is it so difficult for people to grasp how this works?* I thought. *I'd like to see them try not to touch anything.*

Aimee hastened back to where she had abandoned us. "Oh, no, Walter!" She sounded entirely too upset. "How do we get him out?" Aimee asked Troy through the growth.

"I'm not sure. I think I can rip the vines and roots out from the walls, and we can shove him through this narrow part."

"Shove?" I asked. Of course, shove. Why not?

Troy jerked and tugged at the vines and roots, reaching past my legs to get to the ones on Aimee's side. She wrenched the plants too, but with little success.

"Okay, I think that's enough. On the count of three. Aimee, you pull and I'll push."

"What do I do?" I inquired.

Troy laughed and said, "Try to stay on your feet."

Oh, sure. Good. I could do that.

"And from now on shuffle sideways through the tunnels," he added. "One, two, three."

Aimee pulled, Troy shoved, and I stumbled. It was a hurricane of twigs and branches. Every few moments, my arm would catch the side of the wall, reconnecting me to it, but Troy's strength forced me through. Then the tunnel widened again, and we toppled onto one another like a pile of rocks. The binding roots and creepers had faded away.

"Get off me," Aimee grumbled from the bottom of the heap.

"I, uh . . . I'm sorry," I stuttered, extending my hand to help her up. She glared at me, helped herself up, and headed down the tunnel.

Troy patted me on the shoulder and followed after her. Thank goodness we were not in the tunnel much longer. Aimee thrust open a wooden pallet, revealing a cluttered underground laboratory.

## CHAPTER FIVE
# Crinkle-fied

"No way! Is this him?" Grabbed by my hoodie, I was yanked into the lab. "How are you doing, man?" I found myself embraced by a rather spunky young elf with crimped hair that was crazier than mine.

With a muffled tone, I said, "I'm just peachy."

"Awesome! I'm Crinkle." Energy like sunlight burst from his countenance. "I think I have what you need—" He stopped mid-sentence and stared at my feet. He carefully reached down and touched the moss and weeds. "It feels soft and alive." A hurricane of emotions spun across the landscape of his face.

"Crinkle," Aimee said gently, "we have to hurry."

"Right!" He bounded around the room gathering

up items. Crinkle's laboratory had numerous materials and canisters overflowing with unidentifiable elements. Piles of dead plant life, leaves under a microscope, and something bubbling in a tiny pot made up the contents of the room. There were no windows or natural light, just glass lanterns hanging from wooden beams that reinforced the dirt walls.

Just then the earth shook and dirt sprinkled from the ceiling. Something was directly above us. Rhythmic, almost calculated footsteps. Troy held a finger of hush to his lips.

*The Stooges*, I thought.

We waited, clutching our breath inside our chests. Eventually, the brittle ceiling stilled. We remained in unbreakable silence, like we were playing the Quiet Game—the most important round of our lives.

Crinkle moved first. He came up to me with cloth and twine. Before I could protest he was helping me into a jacket, gloves, and a hat. The collared jacket was brown tweed and itched a little around the armpits. The gloves and hat were made of dark gray burlap.

"These will keep you from blossoming everything you touch," he said. Last, he slipped on a bootie that matched the gloves and hat. When my foot reached the ground, nothing happened. Crinkle chuckled. "They work, Aimee. They work!" He put the second bootie on and stepped back to gaze at his masterpiece.

"Now he looks like one of us," Troy said, nodding his head up and down in approval. Then his eyes shifted to the floor and he reached down to pick something up.

"What's this?" he asked.

It was my lion. It must have fallen out of my pocket with all the commotion and costuming.

"That's mine," I said, snatching it from his grip. Troy, Aimee, and Crinkle stepped closer. Why were they so amazed? They looked like they had just seen a two-headed octopus.

I tried to dismiss the trinket. "It's just an old origami lion that has a little quote on the tongue. That's all."

"What does it say?" Aimee asked, eyes twinkling.

"Uh, something like, a cheerful look brings joy to the heart and good news makes for good health." I couldn't tell if they believed me or not, so I pulled out the tab and said, "See?"

My jaw dropped. That's not what it said!

I felt woozy and confused. The lion's tongue said something entirely different. I slowly read it aloud: "Discretion is a life-giving fountain to those who possess it, but discipline is wasted on fools."

Troy's eyes squinted into slivers of suspicion. "What's that supposed to mean?" he barked.

"I don't really know," I stammered. "It said something different before."

"Are you keeping something from us, Walter?" Aimee asked. "Something we need to know?"

"No. I just found this flimsy paper lion in my aunt's truck and somehow the saying has changed."

Crinkle shrugged. "So I guess we should just keep our cool then. You know, be discreet and not stand out. Which is what we need to do with Snot-hook."

"Snot-hook? You mean Ickabod, right?" I asked.

"Aimee calls him Ickabod. The rest of us call him Snot-hook," Crinkle said, rolling his eyes.

Aimee scowled at him, her eyes flickering with anger. "Let's go. Inspection is in a few minutes."

I didn't know what that exchange was about. I was just happy to have some of Aimee's fury directed at someone other than myself.

Back into the tunnels we went. With my new digs, I only had to be careful not to touch anything with my face. That wasn't too hard. We came out of the tunnel through a facade of parched foliage, right behind an outdoor fireplace blocking the view of our exit. Out ahead of us were hoards of Fantaisies migrating down the cobble steps.

"Don't talk to anyone, Walter," Crinkle whispered. "You never know who is a Stooge."

"But I thought they were different than your people."

"No, man. They are our people. They're the ones who have stopped thinking for themselves. They have no creativity left in them. They're zoned-out drudges who only do exactly what Snot-hook tells them to do."

"How do you know who's a Stooge and who isn't?"

"Well, besides their somewhat zombie-like persona, a tiny green check mark appears on their right hand. Like Snot-hook is checking people off a list or something. Crazy stuff, man."

My thoughts were spinning through my head like the vortex roller coaster at last year's summer fair.

"Is that why most of you wear gloves?" I asked.

"Yes, and that's why you have a pair too. Also, because you can't—"

"—touch anything. I know, I know."

Our pace quickened with only minutes remaining. We hoisted ourselves over a small garden wall to save time. When I landed, my bootie snagged on something. Cautious not to tear the bottom I was gingerly loosening the fabric when Troy bashed right into me.

"Oh, sorry, Walter," he said, his fingerless gloved hand pulling me upright.

Oh, no! Did I tear the bootie? I felt a tug on my foot when I hit the ground. Or did I? I couldn't remember clearly. There wasn't a trail of grass as I ran. Thank heavens!

A flagstone courtyard opened up before us. Fantaisies were pouring in like batter into a mixer. A stone stage was mounted in the center, probably meant to hold weddings and other joyous occasions. Atop it stood three elves, one wearing gloves, the others not. I strained to see the adorned check marks, but at this distance I couldn't make out much. There were boulders and built-in benches to sit down, yet everyone remained standing at attention. Aimee, Crinkle, and Troy stood in front of me as my shield.

This place must have been beautiful in its time. I pictured ladies in summer dresses relaxing at delicate bistro tables and gentlemen in vests and bow ties holding cups of coffee. And all of them surrounded by hanging, brightly petaled plants and yellow verbena flowers growing amid the cracks of the flagstone. Maybe a game of Ping-Pong . . .

Lost in my daydream, I hadn't noticed the taller man land on the platform. He surveyed the crowd, inspecting us. I stepped closer to my guardians and sunk down behind them.

An unbearable hush imprisoned the crowd. He turned to face us and I beheld his gnarled face and enormous hooked nose. Snot-hook!

## CHAPTER SIX

# Rhetorical Rule Book

"Lucille, please," demanded the bent-nosed man. He held the lapels of his plum-colored formal outdoor coat alongside his puffed-out chest. Hanging from his neck was a corked bottle containing some kind of clear liquid.

Two Stooges entered the courtyard, clutching the arms of a sheepish girl. She looked down and took small, quick steps. She had coral-blonde hair, dainty features, and was entirely unassuming. What could she have possibly done?

At the sight of her, Crinkle's back stiffened.

"Pretty little Lucille," Snot-hook said, sneering. "Would you like to tell the people what my Stooges found you doing this morning?"

Her eyes flashed up at him as teardrops dripped down her cheeks. Then her shoulders heaved and she hung her head.

"Oh, come on," Snot-hook said. "It's pretty simple. Lucille here broke a rule." He leaned into her personal space. "Didn't you?" His sarcasm was as thick as Aunt Cecelia's oatmeal.

I wanted to punch his smug, beaked nose. *Bubbling.*

Peering through the gap between Crinkle's and Aimee's shoulders, I saw Snot-hook clasp his bony hand around the bottle.

"Lucille violated Rule Number 19. Who can tell me what Rule Number 19 is?" he asked, surveying the crowd. Snot-hook's squinty stare rested on Crinkle. I did my best to shrink in size.

Crinkle shook, seemingly out of rage, not fear. He swallowed hard. Then, as instructed, he said, "Rule Number 19 states that there will be no dressing up in bright colors. Only tones of brown, gray, black, and white are to be worn at all times. Presented in a monochromatic fashion as to encourage unity, not envy." Subtle disdain was laced through every syllable.

"Very good. So you will not be surprised when I show you this." Snot-hook pulled a vivid red-and-yellow flowered dress out of a burlap bag. The crowd gasped. He circled around to be sure the entire group got a good look.

"Pretty Lucille had this dress on this morning in her house. When a Stooge happened to pass by her window, she was dancing around. Dancing is the second offense." Snot-hook paced back and forth in front of Lucille and then lifted the bottle from around his neck.

"No," Crinkle said under his breath and took a step forward. Aimee grabbed his arm.

"And what happens to little elves who do not follow the rules? They have to take their medicine." Snot-hook uncorked the bottle.

Crinkle lunged forward, only to get yanked back by the strong arm of Troy. I liked Crinkle, and Crinkle was mad, which made my anger bubbles fizz up.

Lucille didn't even put up a fight. With all eyes locked on her, she raised a tiny hand of calm in our direction and stepped toward Snot-hook. Salty tears ran down her powder-pink cheeks as he poured the water into Lucille's mouth. She looked dazed, and the light flew out of her eyes.

I suddenly felt very parched, as if I had eaten a dry loaf of bread in the desert. What was he doing to her? I tried to squeeze past Aimee, who elbowed me in the chest, stopping me cold.

"Discretion," she whispered.

Discretion was a life-saving fountain. That's what the lion said. I slinked back behind my three buffers.

"Take her away to the room," Snot-hook demanded, taking a swig of the bottle himself and then returning it to its suspended resting place around his neck. Looking over the flock of Fantaisies, he inquired, "Is there anyone else who would like to think for themselves today?"

Everyone was silent, marred only by a few sounds of shuffling feet.

He pointed to an older, bearded elf. "What is Rule Number 42?"

The elf confidently said, "Rule Number 42 states we may water our gardens between 12:00 p.m. and 12:03 p.m. only, so as to conserve water, sir."

Snot-hook continued his pointing game. "Rule Number 10?"

"Rule Number 10 states we are allowed to read books chosen by our divine leader Ickabod Von Snot-hook to maintain solidarity of thought," a snooty elf replied. I'm sure he added the "divine."

"Rule Number 29?"

"Rule Number 29 states we will walk in an upright, poised manner; no skipping or prancing about for everyone's physical safety," said a shy lady elf.

"Rule Number 57?"

"Rule Number 57 states we will pronounce words clearly in a formal speech pattern of complete sentences; no rhyming of words or filler words such as 'um' or 'huh.' This will aid in more effective communication," proclaimed a childlike elf with bronze eyes.

*Huh. I'm not going to do well here*, I thought.

Then Snot-hook's wrinkled finger circled around the group and finally rested upon Aimee. I crept backward into the crowd, away from his focus. A smile floated behind his scowl, peeking out ever so slightly through his black eyes.

*That's odd. Why is he looking at my Aimee like that? I mean, Aimee. Just Aimee. She's not* my *anything.*

He sauntered closer, looked her straight in the eyes and asked, "Rule Number 1?"

I could not see Aimee's face from where I was now crouching. But the words that tumbled out of her mouth were full of sadness, like they were tied to a brick sinking into the ocean.

"Rule Number 1 states," she said, hesitating, "that we are to conform to the likeness of you. Because having drank from the Fountain of Moxie, you are hereby the prime example of discipline and self-control. We will all comply with the following rules and regulations to create a safe and easily definable world." She stood frozen, locking eyes with Snot-hook.

"Excellent," Snot-hook replied. He paused, perhaps escaping to a fond yet obscure memory deep in the filing cabinets of his mind. After a moment, his focus recentered to a spot on the ground just over Aimee's shoulder. The smile behind his scowl was suddenly replaced by an alarming ebony cloud.

Crinkle and Aimee turned toward each other, making brief eye contact, and then continued along Snot-hook's sight line. They probably expected to see me standing there in my so-called disguise, like a buffoon. But what they saw was a small chunk of sea-green, yellow-flowered ground cover that I had left behind.

Discretion.

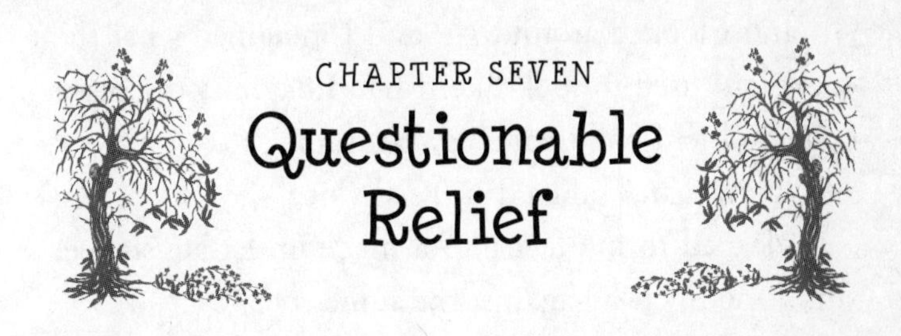

# CHAPTER SEVEN
# Questionable Relief

Stealthily, I squirmed through the crowd and back toward the wall we had scaled. I had to get away from the courtyard inspection. My bootie must have torn. But why did I leave a flower behind? The green had caught my eye when I had backed into the crowd. I'd hoped Snot-hook wouldn't see the evidence of my presence, but he certainly had.

Heart and legs racing, I made my way back to the fireplace escape hatch that led into the tunnels. I ran, swooped, and dodged around cactus-needled weeds, like I was about to make the winning goal in the championship soccer tournament.

Hidden behind the stone flute of the fireplace, I crouched, rolling through my mind's index. What on earth made the plants stay alive sometimes and not others? All I did was stand there during the inspection . . . and I looked around . . . and I imagined what the courtyard used to look like. I had imagined the place come to life. I had imagined. Hmmm.

"Hey, man," said a distressed voice.

I leaped to my feet into a made-up karate stance, smacking my head against the stonework.

Crinkle didn't waste anytime addressing my ridiculous pose. "Still feeling peachy?" he asked as he pulled back the entangled branches to our entrance.

I was in a daze, happy to see him, but I was still unsettled about Lucille and her dress, the rules that no creative soul could possibly keep, and why I kept sprouting permanent bits and pieces of foliage.

Once safely inside the tunnel, Crinkle asked, "How did you get away so fast? I thought for sure Snot-hook had seen you."

"I'm not sure," I said, rubbing the side of my head. "I knew Snot-hook had seen the leafy ground cover. And the word *discretion* ran through my mind like a chant." *My own personal mantra.* "I must have ripped a hole in my bootie," I confessed.

"You don't say," Crinkle replied.

We jogged and shimmied through the tunnels back toward Crinkle's lab.

"Well, we better get your footwear fixed before we go anywhere else," Crinkle suggested. He sounded different. His spunk seemed stifled somehow.

All of a sudden, it was difficult for me to breathe. Maybe it was because the tunnels were musty. Or maybe there wasn't enough oxygen with all the openings covered with various vines and plants.

Once inside the laboratory, a flash flood of questions spilled out of me. "Where's Aimee? Troy? What did Snot-hook do after he saw the flower? Did anyone get sentenced to the gray room? Did Aimee?"

"All right, all right, calm down," Crinkle said as he went to work mending my cloth shoe. "Don't worry about Aimee. She can handle herself."

He went on to tell me that Snot-hook, without taking his eyes off the plant, had made a large check mark–like motion in the air and his Stooges dispersed in all directions. He had then peered back at Aimee with a skeptical frown and Crinkle with a look of mockery. With raised eyebrows on his knotted face, he had said to Troy, "I'm watching you." Then, with a flick of his wrist, a single drop of water fell from his bottle, shriveling the flowery plant into a pathetic pile of dust.

"So I can bring stuff to life and he can . . . kill it?"

"Well, the water from the Fountain of Moxie can, anyway."

"I don't understand this guy!" I exclaimed. "He can wear a royal purple jacket and yet that girl, Lucille, gets punished for her dress?"

At the sound of her name, the remaining light shot out of Crinkle's eyes. He stopped sewing the boot and slumped to the ground. His chest rose and fell in a labored, shallow cadence.

"Uh, what's the matter?" I asked.

"I knew that was going to happen to her." Shadowy anger danced across his face.

"Oh, come on, man. Something crazy like that probably happens at every inspection. It's not like you made her wear the dress."

"No, I didn't make her wear it. But I gave it to her."

"What? Why?" My heart began fluttering wildly, like a trapped butterfly in a jar. Why would Crinkle do that? Was he a Stooge? He had to have known she would get in trouble.

He looked as if he wanted to say something important, but instead he said, "Never mind," and finished stitching up my boot.

I was about to freak out. Why was I here alone with this guy? Why didn't Aimee and Troy come back as well?

A cheerful look and discretion, said the lion. A cheerful look and discretion.

"Soooo, if I'm the one to save you all, we should come up with a plan." I tried to soften my gaze and look . . . well, cheerful.

"Uh, yeah, man. Now that I can hide you again, we are on our way to the old storage shed behind the tennis court. Aimee and Troy will meet up with us there."

I could only hope that was true. Crinkle was the jolliest Fantaisie yet. I didn't want to believe he was already checked off the list.

He tightened the straps that secured his gloves.

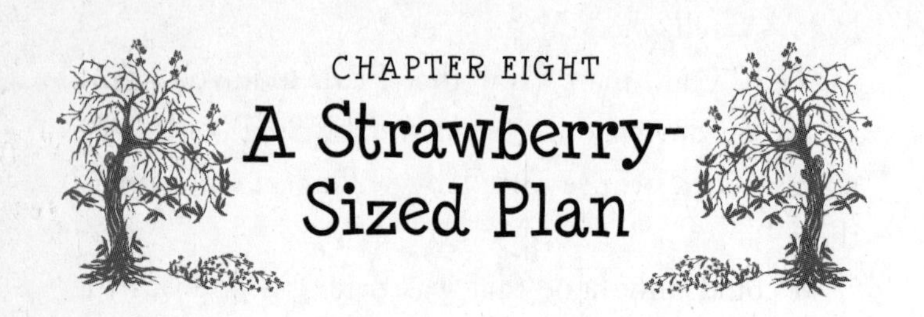

CHAPTER EIGHT

# A Strawberry-Sized Plan

The fossil-like shed was abandoned. Rakes, shovels, trimming sheers—all were rusted and crusty, like they hadn't been used in a decade. Cracked pots roosted on a ledge alongside dusty bags of topsoil longing to be scattered in the garden. The same haze that covered the windows of the so-called chateau settled over the one and only tiny, square windowpane. A faint beam of light was shining on a tall, splintery workbench that stood in the middle.

Uneasiness encircled me. Arriving at the shed alone with Crinkle hadn't eased my anxiety. But then Crinkle grabbed a few empty buckets and flipped them over so we could stand on top of them around the table. The extra buckets indicated Crinkle was at least expecting someone else. I wanted it to be Aimee.

"You've been awfully quiet, Walter," Crinkle said in a hushed tone. "What's up, man?"

"Oh, nothing . . . really," I managed to say. The "really" sounded forced, like I was trying to convince myself as much as him.

Just then there was a rehearsed knock on the door. *Tap, tap, scratch, tap, tap, thud.*

Crinkle hopped down from his bucket and rhythmically knocked back before cracking the door open. His shoulders relaxed, and he opened the door wider to let in his guests.

To my relief and joy, it was Aimee. And Troy.

"Are you all right, Walter?" Aimee asked, her long lashes batting up and down like the wings of a butterfly.

"Uh, I'm okay. I'm really glad to see you though." Again, the "really" sounded forced but for completely different reasons than before. We all stood there in awkward silence.

Finally, Crinkle said, "Okaaay," and stood on his bucket. We all followed suit. Troy rolled out a large map across the workbench, using clay pots to hold down each corner. I was happy Crinkle diverted our attention onto something else besides my overly enthusiastic greeting.

The worn, crumpled parchment mapped out the

entire garden estate. I recognized the hand-drawn courtyard, the fireplace, and even the line of cypress trees we had hid behind. The outline of the chateau's foundation displayed its expansive size. There was the front yard, the crumbling fountain, and the dirt driveway. And parked on it was . . . a blue pickup truck. The only thing in color on the entire map.

"What in the world?" I gasped, staring wide at the aerial view of the truck. "That's my aunt Cecelia's truck. Why is that on the map?"

"Because you've been here before Walter. This map was drawn years ago," Aimee said.

"No, no, I haven't. This is my first time," I said firmly. I was never allowed to go on any sales visits with Uncle Andre and Aunt Cecelia when I spent the summers with them. They would make all their sales before I arrived. I only heard about the people and places they had visited. My mind was foggy and confused. This just doesn't make any sense.

"Let's just move on and get to the plan. He doesn't remember," Troy said.

Crinkle pointed to the east side of the map. "Here are the three fountains. The Fountain of Moxie is on the left, where Snot-hook gets his mind-numbing water. All three fountains have been barricaded in by a towering stone wall."

"Snot-hook put up a wall?" I asked.

"Yup. He didn't want anybody getting to the Fountain of Whimsey, the one in the middle," Crinkle answered.

"And what exactly does the Whimsey fountain do?" I asked, leaning on the edge of one of the small, cracked pots. I'd decided to get some clarification. No more getting dragged around blindly. If I was supposed to "save" these people, I needed to understand what was going on.

Troy let out an annoyed sigh and rolled his eyes.

*Hmm. That's kind of rude. Why is he so irritated by my questions?*

"The Fountain of Whimsey is the fountain of imagination," Crinkle said. "And imagination brings life."

"Well, if that's what the fountain does, what do you need me for?"

"We don't really—" Troy began.

"We need you because none of us possess the Life-power," Aimee interrupted. "You have to dip your hand into the fountain for its powers to be released. You're like a key, Walter."

This was getting kinda ridiculous. How could I possibly be a key to unlock the fountain that's full of imagination? I'd hardly had a chance to use my imagination. I was stuck in this dingy shed with empty pots and canisters calling out for the strawberry or tomato plants that once inhabited them.

"When does my so-called Lifepower come into play? I only get to use it on the Fountain of Whimsey?" I asked.

I looked back and forth between the three faces. No response. Aimee, Crinkle, and Troy were just staring at the pot I was leaning on. I glanced down, then slowly withdrew my hands. But the strawberry plant I had pictured in my mind moments before remained. With yellowish-green leaves with plump, crimson berries, it practically glowed inside the drab shadowy shed. Cool!

"Can we eat them?" Crinkle asked. He reached for the plant and plucked a ripe strawberry from the stem.

"Wait, Crinkle. I don't know if we should," Aimee protested.

"Aimee, it's been too long. And it's right here in my hand."

He put the berry to his lips and bit down, just as Troy said, "I wouldn't do that, Crinkle." There was that same annoyance in his voice as before.

The missing beams of light returned to Crinkle's eyes as he savored the sweet juiciness of the berry. He smiled as wide as an orange slice. "You guys have to try one!"

Both Aimee and I plucked a berry from the plant and ate it. It was the best strawberry I had ever tasted. Somehow, among the shadows and dust, the flavors were elevated to a level that was simply indescribable. Aimee closed her eyes and let the morsel sit on her taste buds.

Our enchanted salivating was interrupted by a pounding fist that shook the workbench. "What are you doing?" Troy scolded. "Did you already forget what happened to Lucille? You know what Snot-hook will do to you if he hears about this."

The three of us snapped to attention. I swallowed the last of my berry, but Aimee carefully placed her leftover berry with leafy stem on the workbench. For the rest of our time in the shed, the strawberry plant was regarded as invisible although it still remained alive and vibrant on the table.

I wasn't sure if Troy's protest was a word of caution or a threat. His tone since the inspection teetered on the edge of harsh.

"Once we tunnel under the stone wall," Troy continued, "and you're inside, Walter, that's when you will use your Lifepower. And only then. We can't have Snot-hook capture you before we get inside the wall."

"We've tunneled most of the way there already in preparation for your arrival. We'll finish tonight," Crinkle added.

"So what happens once we're inside?" I asked cautiously.

"Well, we don't really know. We just have to get you to the Fountain of Whimsey, no matter what happens," Crinkle said as he hopped off his bucket.

Troy began to roll up the map and I had a sudden urge to consult my lion. While sliding my bucket back into its place, I pulled out the lion, peeking at its tongue.

*Beware of false prophets who come*
*disguised as harmless sheep,*
*but are really vicious wolves.*

A lump the size of a grapefruit formed in my throat and I couldn't swallow.

Crinkle or maybe . . . Troy.

I couldn't breathe.

CHAPTER NINE

# Daisy

I sat alone at a wooden dining table inside a dugout beneath a knotted olive tree—the home of Pierre-Louis, Aimee's dad. Aimee wanted to check on him before our sneak attack on Snot-hook. This was our safe haven for the time being.

There were hardly any sounds in Fantaisie, especially in this house. All the animals and insects must have migrated elsewhere, with no real food to eat or water to drink here. I felt so thirsty, like my tongue was made of cotton. I thought about asking for a drink of water but decided against it.

*Oh, what I would give for some grilled salmon with rosemary and thyme, washed down with a glass of sparkling cider*, I thought.

"Walter," Aimee said, appearing from the adjoining room, "my father would like to speak with you."

I dragged my parched body off the chair. I'd never had so many people want to talk to me in my entire life.

To my surprise, Aimee shut the door behind me, leaving me alone in the bedroom with her ill father. He was lying in bed. A lantern on the nightstand illuminated a journal in his craggy hands.

"Please, come in, Walter," Pierre-Louis said, motioning to the wobbly chair beside him. He was as pale as a polar bear. "What have they told you?" he asked groggily.

"Well, sir, uh . . . just that in a short time we'll be tunneling under the wall into Snot-hook's guarded fountain area," I answered. "And that I'm supposed to dip my hand in the Fountain of Whimsey to activate it or something."

"Right, that's what they told you, but what do you want to do?"

"Um . . . I'm not sure what you mean."

"Do you have a different idea, Walter?"

"Well, at the moment I don't really have any. I just want to do whatever is required to stop this monochromatic maniac before my brain gets sucked dry too."

"Ha," was all Pierre-Louis said with a half smile, and then there was a lull.

I clunked back and forth on the uneven legs of the chair, cutting the long silence. Finally, letting out a nervous breath, I said, "Look, I want to help you all out because I get it. I've been there. But I never wanted to do this adventure thing on my own. My uncle—"

"What about the lion?"

"What? Did Aimee tell you?"

"She didn't. I knew you were guided by the lion the first time I saw you." His eyes glistened as if he knew something profound, something my puny mind had yet to grasp.

"How did you know?"

"With the word of the lion comes a decisive, fruitful life and creative imagination. You decided to help us."

Hmm. I had decided that.

The chair creaked as I stood up. I paced back and forth in the dimly lit room. I'd always had a creative imagination. That's what has gotten me in trouble on countless occasions. But the words on the tongue of the lion had helped me stay out of trouble, it seemed, even while using my imagination. I stopped and peered into Pierre-Louis's cloudy eyes.

Before I could speak, he said, "Listen to the words of the lion, Walter. Let it guide you. You have been sent to save us. No one else can. Not Aimee or Crinkle or even strong Troy."

*You have been sent to save us.* His words echoed in my mind.

Pierre-Louis began to look woozy. His eyelids fell closed, then opened again as if he was fighting sleep.

"Thank you," I said and excused myself, returning to the dining area. When I turned around, I pressed my back against the door in surprise. The room was full of Fantaisies holding pots and containers.

"So what's going on?" I asked.

"Apparently, Crinkle has a big mouth," Aimee answered. "Word got out about the strawberries, and they want you to fill their pots with food too. But I don't think it's a good idea, Walter."

*She doesn't think it's a good idea, huh? Well, I think people need to eat.*

"I'll do it. Just one at a time," I said.

One by one, I touched the rim of the jar or bucket and imagined the plant of their choice inside. Within seconds, tomatoes, strawberries, cucumbers, baby spinach, and even a dwarf apple tree blossomed into existence. Some wanted food, while others simply wanted colorful flowers to brighten their homes. They smiled and laughed each time a plant would sprout up. Some even cried—a different kind of crying than my aunt Cecelia's. Their happiness and joy sparkled like fireworks at the county fair.

"How are they supposed to leave here with pots overflowing with color, Walter?" Aimee asked with an air of frustration on her lips. *Geez. Why isn't she excited about this?* My imagination was actually helping these people.

Just then, a bubbly young elf holding a bright yellow daisy spoke up, "Don't worry. We brought burlap sacks to cover them." Handing the flower to Aimee, she said, "This is for your father. I hope it brings joy to his heart." The elf smiled sweetly and left empty-handed—and glove-free. No one in the room had gloves on their hands.

Daisy in hand, Aimee stood there dumbfounded. I didn't think she had thought to give her father a flower. Neither had I, honestly. She stared down at the flower and tears suddenly splashed out of her eyes like an overflowing swimming pool. Before I could offer a word of comfort, she whirled around and slipped inside Pierre-Louis's room.

Then an elderly lady elf slipped through the front door, removing her gloves and tossing them into an already large pile. She zipped across the room and shoved an old coffee canister into my hands.

"Bean sprouts, please," she said.

"Huh, I think coffee beans grow on trees," I said. "This container isn't big enough."

"No, I don't want coffee beans. I want bean sprouts for my soup. I like the crunch."

"Oh, I see."

"That there's the only container I could find," she said, her wrinkly fingers tapping on the side of the can.

"Hey, before I make your bean sprouts, would you mind telling me why there are gloves piled by the door?"

"Oh, nobody enters Pierre-Louis's house without taking off their gloves. He doesn't want any Stooges in here, especially on a day like today. Could you imagine?" she said, chuckling.

Imagine? I had yet to see a green check mark. And today all hands wanting homegrown food were free and clear.

I felt a tug on my sleeve.

"My bean sprouts?" the old lady asked with raised brow and outstretched hand.

"Oh, I'm sorry. Here ya go."

*What would happen if someone refused to remove their gloves?* I wondered.

"Hey, it's time to go!" Troy hollered at me from the front doorway.

I still had a few more containers to fill and I was feeling pretty good about my work here. I had within me the Lifepower, as Aimee called it, and for once in my life, I was making people happy. People other than my aunt and uncle, who were happy up until the unexpectedly awful had occurred.

I answered back from across the room, "Troy, come in and take a look at all the plants. You gotta try something to eat."

"No, Walter, we don't have time for that. Get Aimee and let's go!"

Apparently, Troy's grumpy meter had reached full capacity.

Aimee came out of Pierre-Louis's room. A softness had settled upon her cheekbones. She gazed at me with a kindness I had never before seen in her eyes. There was a moment between us, I think. Maybe she was just thankful, or maybe she had decided she "liked" me . . . too. Maybe.

"Uh . . . Troy's here," was all that stumbled out of my mouth. "But he won't come in."

"Oh, he never comes in. Always in a hurry," she said.

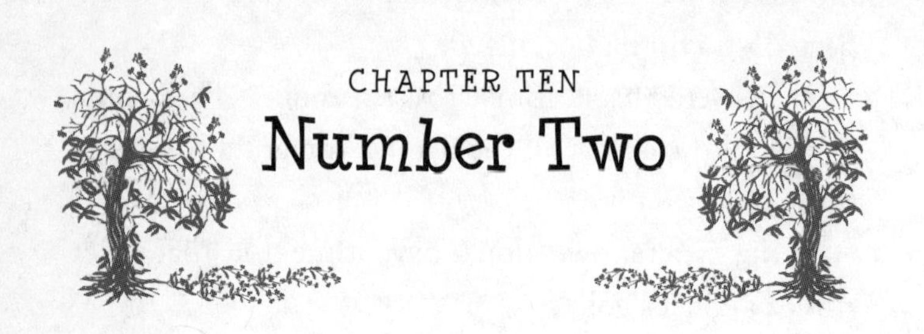

CHAPTER TEN

# Number Two

Troy hurried Aimee and I along in the direction of the fountains, through brittle brush and weeping trees to an obscure tunnel opening, behind a rock garden wall. Several feet away stood a rickety, rotten gazebo. *Probably once a nice place to have an eggs Benedict brunch on a crisp morning*, I thought.

When we were inside, we weaved through the darkness. I preferred the soft, overcast light of the day compared to the ghostly light of the tunnel.

*Shadows. Dark. Shadows.*

We came into a dug-out cavern, directly beneath the once-charming gazebo. Crinkle and several other Fantaisies crowded into the hollow, carrying shovels, picks, and spades.

"Hey, guys. We're almost to the fountains. Only have a few feet to go, directly under the wall, and then up about three feet," Crinkle explained. "I see you're wearing all your protective gear, Walter."

"Uh, yeah. I see you have your gloves on too," I said.

"It makes it easier to shovel the dirt," he replied.

*Beware of false prophets who come disguised . . .*

"Speaking of easier, I was thinking. I probably should take off my gloves before we go into Snot-hook's lair so I'm ready for the fountain," I said.

"It's best you leave them on, don't you think?" Troy said. "Don't want to give us away too early."

He scolded me like I was a dim-witted child. Well, I am a child, technically, but dim-witted I am not.

*. . . As harmless sheep but are really vicious wolves.*

"Troy, what's up with you lately?" Aimee asked. "Walter is here to help us."

Troy looked down at his feet, kicked at the dirt, and then skulked down the tunnel.

"Okay, we better get back to work," Crinkle said, nodding at the other Fantaisies who disappeared into the dark tunnel. He turned to follow, but then looked back at me and said, "Hey man, it's been totally crazy since you got here. But I'm super glad you're here." He was gone before I could respond.

What? I couldn't figure this guy out. Did he want to be my pal? Or did he want to hand me over as a sacrifice to the nefarious Snot-hook? Good grief. I soon became quite aware of the fact that Aimee and I were the only two left in the underground room. She was staring at me, so I stared back at her.

"Are you going to hit me?" I asked with a deadpan expression.

She burst out laughing, a joyful release that echoed through the emptiness. Almost like when a baby starts giggling uncontrollably at a dog.

I couldn't believe it! I had made her laugh! I mean, I'd always been funny—witty anyway—but to get this girl to let out an emotion other than carbonated anger . . . I had to be pretty good.

Soon, her laughter faded into sobbing. I panicked for a moment. What was I supposed to do with this? This is the exact opposite of what happened with Aunt Cecelia. Her tears turned into laughter.

Both occurrences were entirely too uncomfortable. I scrunched my eyes closed and imagined a beautiful red flower, like the first one I held in my hand when I arrived in the garden. The flower sprung up right next to my shoe. I picked it and handed it to Aimee.

"Here, this is for you," I said with a smile.

She accepted the flower with a soft grin and a

sniffle, then sat down in the dirt. I sat down next to her. Twirling the flower in front of her face, she said, "I used to do this when I was little. Then I would put it in my hair." She wiggled the stem into one of her braids. "How's it look?"

"I, uh . . . well, it looks fine, I mean good, I guess. It looks good." Smooth as frosting on a cake. Uncle Andre was smooth with my aunt. He would sing to her quirky made-up songs, write her poems, and give her flowers. I didn't know whether I'd be able to do all that, but since I had this Lifepower in me, the least I could do is grow the girl a flower.

"I'm sorry, Walter," Aimee continued, wringing her hands. "It's all been so hard to understand. I mean, why did Ickabod drink so much from the Fountain of Whimsey? Why did he have to turn into such a mean person?" She spoke as if she had seen it firsthand.

I almost asked her if she had, but I thought it best to keep my mouth shut for the moment.

"And now you're here, and I haven't been all that nice to you. Sometimes I think having to follow all these rules all the time has made me mean, like Ickabod." She hung her head and made swirls with her finger in the dirt.

I knew now was the time to talk, but I wasn't quite sure if the words about to slip out of my mouth would be any help. "Uh, well, I get it. Strict rules and no creativity are the worst. I think anybody would be a bit cranky being bossed around all the time."

"Yeah, I guess you're right," she said as the weighty sadness clung to her face. Something else was bothering her. *Do I ask or just wait? I'll wait about ten seconds. One-one thousand. Two-one thousand. Three-one thousand. Four-one—*

"I'm worried about my father—"

*Phew! She dished her feelings on her own.*

"He's brokenhearted, Walter. Torn up about the state of his land and people. I'm not sure how to help him."

"Did the daisy help?" I asked

"Oh, Walter, he was overjoyed. I hadn't seen him smile in months. Thanks for breathing life into that daisy."

I just nodded and grinned.

"What about your parents, Walter? What are they like?" Aimee asked.

"Uh, well . . . Actually, some crazy stuff happened and my parents died. That's why I live with my aunt and uncle."

"I'm so sorry, Walter. You don't seem too upset about it, though. If I lost my dad, it would take me decades to recover," Aimee replied.

"Well, I wasn't close to my parents like you are with your father. I never saw much of them, and when I did I was lectured about my latest blunder. They were practically strangers."

"What happened to them?"

"My father had a tendency to drink too much. He choked on the olive and toothpick from his martini glass." I shot out of the starting gate with a bang.

Aimee looked at me, wide-eyed and, perhaps, flabbergasted. But it was true.

"Wait, it gets better," I said. "My mother was consumed with her appearance and all things material. One day, while crossing the street, her designer high heel got stuck in the metal grid of the sewer drain. Apparently, she refused to leave it behind, and it began to sprinkle. The sprinkles turned into rain, then hail. A policeman had to pry her hands from the shoe, dragging her kicking and screaming out of the weather. She caught a cold, which turned into pneumonia, and she never recovered."

"You've got to be kidding me," Aimee responded.

"Nope. That's what the policeman reported anyway, but I don't doubt it."

Eyes wide, she shook her head back and forth. "So, now you live with your aunt and uncle?"

"Yup, their truck is the blue one on the map. So,

you see, I haven't been here beforc. Maybe it was my aunt or Uncle Andre who visited in the past."

"Andre. Hmmm . . . sounds familiar." Aimee paused, lost in thought.

Did she know something about my uncle or was she just being an active listener?

I had a sudden urge to share the words of the lion with her. Perhaps it could offer some insight. I removed the lion from my pocket, and Aimee's eyes lit up like lightning bugs at dusk. As she leaned in, I unraveled the lion's tongue and read aloud, "Two are better than one. If one falls down, his friend can help him up. Pity the man who falls and has no one to help him up!"

*I've found my number two*, I thought.

CHAPTER ELEVEN

# Make a Wish

Troy popped his head into the hollow. "Let's go, lovebirds! We don't have time for your little romantic chats."

Aimee and I exchanged a quick, awkward glance. My cheeks felt hot as we trotted after Troy through the narrow tunnel that twisted and curved around the root structures of trees and a few boulders here and there, until we came to the end. Instead of gold and jewels, chunks of concrete and piles of dirt marked the spot of our wanna-be treasure hunt.

The Fantaisies glanced upward. "One more swing of this pickax, and we'll be through the floor of Snot-hook's territory," Crinkle whispered. "We should be directly behind the Fountain of Whimsey, if I calculated correctly."

That fountain and I were destined to meet. I felt like I had no say in the matter. After the impromptu gardening session at Pierre-Louis's home, I knew I could bring things to life.

That wasn't the part that worried me. Who—or what—was waiting up there? The thought gave me the urge to pee my pants.

Crinkle arched his pickax up over his head.

I looked at Aimee, who looked at Troy, who looked at me and nodded a silent "let's do this."

The pickax crashed into the remaining layer of dirt. The debris plummeted to the ground, barely missing us and adding to the heaps of earthy treasures.

When the dust settled, everyone eyeballed me.

*Oh, great. They're gonna shove me up there by myself,* I thought. Uncle Andre's adventures always felt like fun fairy tales when heard from the comfort of the front porch. This moment, however, had a whole other feeling—fear. What was happening to my itching curiosity? I felt no need to scratch.

"Walter," Aimee whispered, "Troy will go first, then Crinkle, then you, and then I'll follow behind you."

*Good. Two are better than one,* I thought. *So four must be better than two.*

Troy heaved himself up and through the jagged opening and pulled Crinkle through next. Crinkle's gloved hand reached down, grabbed mine, and hauled me up.

Once inside the stone and concrete enclosure, I saw a bronze-colored stone fountain. Its round basin was half-filled with water and sat on a square pedestal directly in front of us and to the right of a huge pile of rocks. Adjacent to the pile of rocks was another fountain, identical to the first, except it was full to the brim with water. Undoubtedly, the Fountain of Moxie.

At once, I was unbelievably thirsty. Each nervous swallow was constrained as if by a mouthful of smooth peanut butter.

"Psst!" I spun around to our tunnel. Aimee was looking up at me, head cocked, with an expression of "I can't believe you forgot me." I heaved her up to join us behind the fountain.

No Snot-hook or other Fantaisies in sight. That was strange.

Crinkle was shaking his head and making exaggerated hand gestures. I had no idea what he was trying to say.

"This is the wrong fountain," Aimee whispered.

*That's right, the Fountain of Whimsey was the middle fountain.* I stepped back to get a better look. I could only see two fountains, one on each side of a huge pile of rocks. Wow, it was like an eleven-year-old's dream come true—a heap of kicking rocks.

"The Fountain of Whimsey must be buried underneath," I said. We dashed to the pile and began carefully plucking the rocks off one at a time so as to maintain our quiet, incognito status.

We were in the process of making a new pile from those rocks when I realized Troy had disappeared.

"Where did Troy go?" I asked.

"He's our look-out. He went to locate Snot-hook and report back to us if he is coming this way."

"He should be helping us. He's the one with the muscles," I muttered.

Crinkle shrugged and continued gathering stones.

With crabby Troy gone, I decided to take off my gloves and utilize my Lifepower. Maybe I could help us get this done faster. Crinkle saw me remove the gloves and his eyes squinted with curiosity. When I touched the pile of rocks with my bare hand, they were suddenly covered with dirt, olive-colored weeds, and puffy white dandelions. For a moment, I held the image of rocks and weeds in my mind. I released my touch, and the new growth stayed, just how I imagined it.

I picked a dandelion and handed it to Aimee. "Make a wish."

Aimee knew the drill. She blew all the seedlings off

the stem, and we watched as they floated about. Some seeds landed on rock and would consequently die there. Others landed in good soil, where a dandelion would take root. One seed fluttered past my nose and drew my attention back to the cluster of rocks, now padded with dirt and plant life. With a wink at Aimee and Crinkle, I pushed on the peak of the pile. It tumbled to the ground with barely a sound.

Aimee and Crinkle smiled, and all three of us circled around to one side and shoved large chunks of the pile to the ground. Soon we saw the inside of the fountain. I expected to see mud in the round basin as the glorious water bubbled up from inside, but all that was there were more dry rocks—no water.

CHAPTER TWELVE

# Secret Rain

*Where in the world is the water I'm supposed to dip my hand into? This is not good.* I felt queasy. Stinky fumes filled my nostrils and made my eyes water.

Crinkle and Aimee desperately scooped and yanked out clumps of grass, dirt, and rocks in search of any evidence of water, but there wasn't any.

This was crazy. We should have had a plan B.

Hasty footsteps headed straight for us. *This is it*, I thought. *We're about to be force-fed the Moxie water and sentenced to the gray room where our brains will be sucked dry.* I spun around ready to face the ugly, vehement Ickabod Von Snot-hook. To my surprise, it was Troy racing toward us.

"Snot-hook knows we're here. We have to go!" he shouted. Troy headed for the tunnel without stopping. Seconds later, the Stooges stomped into view like a marching band at halftime. Stooges circled around Aimee, Crinkle, and me, some glaring, some smiling, but all far too satisfied to have us for company. Although, I didn't think they were about to offer us a grape soda and peanut butter cookies—my favorite. No, they served us their leader.

Snot-hook strolled into the clearing—a most disagreeable snack. *Man, is he ugly*, I thought. Even uglier than the first time I saw him.

"Hahaha!" Snot-hook bellowed. "So this is the little magical boy who's been creating color all over my world."

Crinkle stepped in front of me. His brow was in a tight V, a similar expression to the one he had when Lucille was on display at the inspection.

"Oh, please, like you can protect him," Snot-hook mocked. "You couldn't even protect your pathetic sweetheart Lucille, could you?"

*Sweetheart? Oooohhhh, that's why Crinkle gave her the dress. Maybe he's not a wolf in disguise after all.*

Crinkle tensed and leaned forward, a bull about to charge.

"Discretion," was all I could squeak out. He heeded my word—well, the word of the lion anyway.

Snot-hook looked me over with beady black eyes. "This is just brilliant. You came to me. I didn't even have to find you. You're awfully puny, though. I can't imagine the task would have been difficult."

*Imagine? You can't imagine it*, I thought. *Catching me would have been as easy as getting spilled cranberry juice out of the ivory sofa—that's right, not so easy.* My defense argument was rising up within me, even though my case wasn't too profound.

He glanced at the fountain beside us. "The Fountain of Whimsey is all dried up. How sad for you. Let me guess, you planned to dip your hand in the water, activate its power, and then everything would magically come back to life."

How did he know that?

"Did you really think it would be that simple?" he asked.

No, I didn't, but up until this point I hadn't had much say. Geez.

Then Snot-hook's wretched expression softened ever so subtly. He was looking straight through me to the quiet elf girl frozen behind me.

"How nice of you to come and visit me," he said to Aimee. "It's been a long time."

What in the world was he talking about? Aimee had been to see him? Here?

He must have seen the look of confusion on my face. He chuckled and tossed his head back. "Oh, I see," he said. "Your new buddy doesn't know, does he?"

*Know what?*

Crinkle turned and looked me in the eye. He seemed to know too.

"Aimee and I—" Snot-hook began.

"No, don't," Aimee interrupted. She rushed right up to him and peered into that wrinkled face. "I beg you, Ickabod. Don't say anything more. He doesn't need to know."

Snot-hook glared at her, then ripped the flower from her hair, crumpling it in his fist and tossing it on the ground. Aimee's shoulders heaved with a sigh.

Geez, buddy! I almost ran to pick up the flower but then I thought, *I'll just grow her another one.*

With a huff, Snot-hook took her hand in his. Aimee tensed and hung her head. But she did not pull her hand away. Tears speckled her cheeks like sprinkling rain.

Then somehow I knew. And I didn't like it. And I especially did not understand it. My thoughts began to spin, as if Aimee's teardrops were the beginning of a violent storm. I didn't want to know the whole story.

*Bubbling . . .*

But Ickabod—I mean Snot-hook—wanted me to know. "Aimee and I were best friends. We were in love."

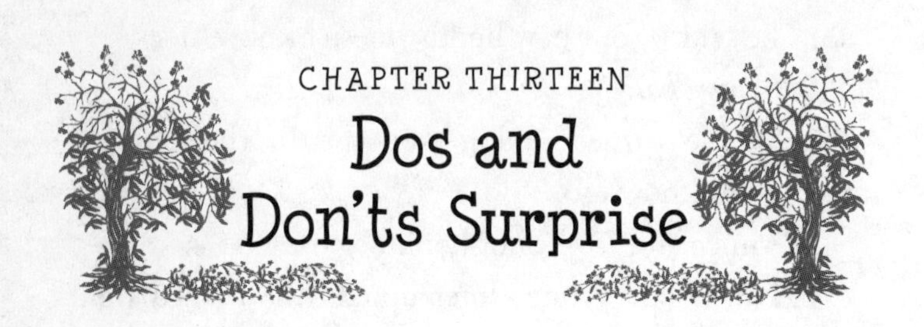

CHAPTER THIRTEEN

# Dos and Don'ts Surprise

I couldn't quite grasp what was happening. My anger bubbles were starting to roll. Yet all I could think was, *Why would Aimee love this guy? First of all, he's old and worn-out looking. Second of all, he is killing people's imaginations. Third of all, . . . well, there's no need for a third of all. Those two reasons are good enough.*

"From the time we were little, we were inseparable," Snot-hook continued. "We dreamed that the glorious Fantaisie lands would be overflowing with life and happiness. And once we were old enough we would get married, and I would become the leader of the Fantaisie peoplc. But . . ."

He looked down at Aimee, took her by the shoulders, and spun her around to face me. "Why don't you tell the rest of the story."

"Walter, I am so sorry," Aimee said. "I didn't want you to think poorly of me."

"Come on, Aimee. Tell him what you did," Snot-hook pressed.

All the words of the lion flooded the sandy beach of my thoughts. Yet I did not have, nor did I want to give, a cheerful look, and this wasn't good news.

*Bubbling . . .*

And, apparently, there was no need for discretion. How could I be such a fool? They all knew there was more to the story. They just left me out like a painting in the rain. Dripping and pathetic.

*Bubbling . . . shadows . . .*

Aimee—not Snot-hook or Crinkle or Troy—had disguised herself as a harmless sheep, but she was really a snarly wolf.

*Bubbling . . . shadows . . . darkness . . .*

*Two are better than one. . . .*
*Pity the man who falls*
*and has no one to help him up!*

I was to be pitied, paint dripping from my canvas. No more number two. Just *numero uno.* This is how it's always been. A lot of demands and rules with no explanation, and me all alone in the controlled chaos. Except for when I was with Uncle Andre, but he was not here!

*Bubbling . . . shadows . . . dark . . . BURST!*

"I've had enough!" I yelled, tearing off my jacket and hat and ripping off the booties.

Crinkle's eyes were as round as frisbees. He gawked at me, partly, I thought, because of my newfound courage and partly because I had torn his creation up and thrown it to the ground.

"Listen, old man," I said, taking a step of faith toward Snot-hook. Slivers of green and yellow moss traveled through the cracks of the concrete. I stood in a puddle of color and felt proud to let the various shades shine.

Aimee looked like a startled kitty cat. The Stooges shifted and glanced at one another, their expressions laced with shock and panic. And Snot-hook, for once, looked confused.

"You think you can boss us around with your dos and don'ts," I scolded.

Aimee shook her head back and forth—a warning I ignored.

"We have within us something you don't: imagination. That brings life and light to the world."

With a bellowing laugh, Snot-hook retorted, "What do you mean 'old man'? Looks like your imagination has shuffled your deck, my tiny friend. I'm only a few years older than yourself."

*That's all he took from my speech? The fact that he was old? You've got to be kidding me.* I laughed awkwardly, a bit confused myself. "This is a joke, right? I mean, how can you be young, yet be all wrinkly and have that icky, large nose?"

"No, Walter, he doesn't know," Aimee said. Snot-hook snapped a suspicious glare at Aimee.

*Oh, goody. Now, he's the one who gets the pleasure of an unwanted surprise.* "Wait a minute, he doesn't know what?" I asked Aimee.

"He doesn't know he's aged," Crinkle whispered.

Snot-hook reached up and felt around his face. "This is ludicrous," he stated. He marched over to the Fountain of Moxie and peered into the rippling water.

"I look more and more handsome every day. Take a look for yourself." He waved us toward the fountain.

I didn't want to go near that water. But that missing-in-action, itchy-itch-itching curiosity was now tossing around my insides like flapjacks on the griddle. I needed to know what he was talking about.

Crinkle and I locked eyes and inched toward the fountain together. The Stooges closed in around us like a rubber band cinching a bag of potato chips, forcing Aimee to accompany us, whether she wanted to or not.

Steering clear of the poisonous water, all three of us leaned over the edge just far enough to get a glimpse of Snot-hook's reflection.

My breath sucked up into me like a vacuum.

I couldn't believe what I saw.

## CHAPTER FOURTEEN
# You're Ugly

Dancing in the gentle swells of the water was Snot-hook's reflection, but it was not a mirror image. Staring back at us from the Moxie water was a young and somewhat handsome guy. I wouldn't have recognized that face as ever belonging to Snot-hook.

Crinkle and I both looked back and forth, and back and forth, between the image floating in the water and the guy standing before us. Crinkle seemed to recognize the young face. His back and forths were more of a comparison, where as my back and forths were full of amazement and wonder.

Aimee's face scrunched up and she stared at the face in the water with longing. Gobs of emotion spilled out of her eyes. *Oh, geez, not more crying*, I thought. I was seeing the same thing she was and I didn't feel the need to cry. I thought, *This is way cool. This is the kind of crazy stuff adventures are made of.*

I recalled how I had stood up to the fruit man in defense of my kicking rock. With that same boldness I blurted out, "You do know that's not what you look like, right?"

Snot-hook shot a thorny glare in my direction and stepped back from the fountain. Aimee watched the reflection slipping away and tried to grab a hold of it, but Crinkle yanked her hand back before she touched the water.

"How dare you!" Snot-hook bellowed. His stiff, cold shell was starting to crack. I didn't want to discover what would happen when the lid blew off his pressure cooker.

This was the part of adventures I didn't much care for.

Crinkle, Aimee, and I huddled together, keeping our mouths shut for the time being.

"You're delusional, you itsy-bitsy, pathetic boy," Snot-hook said to me. His hooked beak was so close that the large pores were like deep dents of a waffle, full of butter and molasses. Yuck.

*If he refers to me as "little" one more time . . .*

Just then, Aimee located her voice, and the sound that came out was familiar to me. Her words were flavored with attitude—the same attitude she had when I first met her. I could only hope that her hostility in this moment would result in her punching Snot-hook in his syrupy nose.

"Stop calling him little," she demanded. "You may not believe him, but will you believe me?"

"What are you talking about?" Snot-hook asked.

For a long, uncomfortable moment she absorbed his appearance like a sponge; then she inhaled and said, "You're ugly."

She didn't have to punch him in the face. Her words hit hard. "That Moxie water is making you old and worn out," she continued, "and you can't even see your true reflection. All that was once handsome is gone."

His right eye twitched like a crazy person. "Please, I'm even better looking than I was before. With every chug of the Moxie water, I get more handsome and have more power than ever."

"No, that's not true," Aimee said flatly. "With each drink, you get older and more grotesque."

Each word that trickled out of Aimee's mouth made Snot-hook writhe in fury. His eyelids twitched like he had just hiked through a sandstorm. His mouth puckered and his cheek muscles jerked around like a volcano about to erupt, spewing burning lava all over the defenseless landscape.

But Aimee didn't seem to mind. She kept going. I think she felt the need to get this off her probably broken heart.

"And the more horrid you look on the outside, the more humdrum you are on the inside. Or maybe it's the other way around. Your tedious rules have made you . . . *boring*!" She really pounded out that last word. As if she knew that word would aggravate him to his boiling point.

And it did.

He stepped right into Aimee's personal space and breathed what I was sure was nasty smelling breath in her face. "What's Rule Number 12, Aimee?"

"I don't care about your rules anymore."

"Oh, really? Well, I'll remind you what it says." His frigidness was returning. "Rule Number 12 states that all comments regarding the nature and character of your leader, Ickabod Von Snot-hook, will be positive and uplifting so as to encourage him in his challenging position as leader."

Without further ado, he lifted the ever-present vile from around his neck and uncorked it. "For you to drink, my dear," he said to Aimee. "It will give you a taste of your own medicine."

*What is this lunatic talking about? What medicine?* I was incredibly confused. Confusion seems to be a theme running through the story of my life.

*Darkness . . . shadow . . .*

Snot-hook reached for Aimee. In a flash, Crinkle and I pulled her back and shielded her behind us.

Snot-hook laughed. Okay, he had laughed before, but not quite like this. The laughter consisted of creepy I'm-about-to-flatten-you laughter, dispersed with outbursts of hysterical, delirious chuckles.

*Oh, great, he's losing his mind*, I thought. Just what we needed: to be trapped inside these stone walls, surrounded by stubborn rule-followers. In that moment, Snot-hook belonged in a comic book, the part where the evil villain has no other plans but desperation and is about to snap.

*Bubble . . . bubble . . . bubble . . . bubble . . . bubble . . .*

My anger bubbles came rushing into me like the jets in a hot tub. Snot-hook was going to make Aimee drink the Moxie water sloshing around in the vial. I couldn't let that happen. For her sake and for Crinkle (who was the only one left to be my number two, my friend).

*Bubble . . . bubble . . . POP!*

I lunged toward Snot-hook, smacking the Moxie water from his hand. The bottle shattered on the ground.

I expected chaos to break out, and we could fight our way to the tunnel, but nobody moved. Snot-hook stopped laughing, which I would have welcomed a few seconds ago but now the silence was agonizing, like the awkward quiet after a bad joke.

Finally, Snot-hook raised his hand in the air and made the swooping check mark sign.

Then chaos commenced.

Shouting Stooges charged us. They instantly grabbed ahold of Aimee and Crinkle. One nitwit was about to pounce on me, and I had to think fast. I closed my eyes and imagined the Stooge wrapped in vines. I waited a millisecond before I opened my eyes again. When I did, a practically mummified Stooge stood before me. Vines had grown through the cracks in the stone floor. Perfect! It worked, and I didn't even have to be touching him.

I dodged and ducked a couple more tackles from the mind-numbed Stooges. Then I grew a puffy, mint-green garlic plant in the path of another, who tripped and tumbled to the floor. All the while, I made my way to the tunnel entrance.

*Aw, geez. I'm forgetting someone.*

I spun around and visualized a hedge (a look-alike to the one I had experimented with earlier in the front yard), and instantly the tall hedge grew up underneath the Stooge holding Crinkle. The hedge lifted the stooge off his feet and into the air, and Crinkle slipped from his grasp. Okay, he was free.

Aimee was next. Despite the deceit and all, I

couldn't leave her behind. But before I could picture anything in my mind, the Stooges dragged her toward the hallway that Snot-hook had entered through.

To my utter shock, Crinkle was sneaking up behind them.

"Crinkle!" I shouted.

He turned, looked me in the eye, and mouthed, "Lucille."

I got the picture.

I wanted to go with him, to help save her, but a pack of Stooges were closing in on me fast.

On my way to the tunnel, I sprouted up roots and tiny bushes with each step. Booby traps, of sorts, for my pursuers.

As I hopped into the escape tunnel, I caught a glimpse of Snot-hook. He had not moved a step in any direction. He just stood there, surrounded by life, plants, and color, like a dingy pot at the end of a rainbow. But he wasn't filled with gold. He stared at me over the top of the hedge with narrow eyes and pursed lips. The hatred in his eyes was startling. He hated the plants, the color, the life, and, most of all, me.

CHAPTER FIFTEEN

# A Chicken and a Hideout

Running through the scarcely lit passage, I had no idea what I would do next. The two elves I had allowed to guide me this far were now worse off than when I'd arrived—stuck in the dark, gray quarters of Ickabod Von Snot-hook's lair.

My third tour guide had run away like a big chicken. Where could Troy have gone?

I wanted to stop running and see what the lion had to say about it all. But I wouldn't take that chance. My running was more like that of a dance, on my tiptoes trying to touch the least amount of dirt as I could. Weeds and roots came to life and shrank back down again.

Smashing the bottle was stupid. All Snot-hook had to do was get another one and refill it at the Fountain of Moxie—the very fountain we were standing next to. What was I thinking, showing off like that? Letting those unruly bubbles get the best of me . . . again. Now Aimee had been caught by the Stooges, not rescued by me, a so-called superhero.

Shouts from stomping Stooges trailed behind me. There was enough distance between us, for now.

What would Uncle Andre do? At that thought, my lungs felt like a balloon full of water. There was so much pressure I could hardly breathe. This adventure thing was even more overwhelming than I could have ever imagined.

And Uncle Andre always appeared so confident in his storytelling, like a caped crusader in Saturday morning cartoons. From the bottom of my heart, I wished my uncle was there with me.

*But he's not here, so get over it*, I told myself.

Well, there was one other elf who could possibly help me: Pierre-Louis.

After all, back in his room he had asked, "What are your ideas, Walter?" And he'd said, "You have been sent to save us." Those two sentences were popcorn at the movies, a perfect combination. I had to find my way back to his home without a trail of Stooges accompanying me. I zigzagged through the last part of the tunnel. I was almost to the cavern, then I would be out in the overcast light of the day. *I'm going to need a place to hide out*, I thought.

Just then, someone stepped in my path, and we both went crashing to the ground. Sparks of green, yellow, and white flowers and plants bounced along with our flailing limbs into the cavern beneath the gazebo.

I scurried to my feet, waving the dust from my eyes. Oh, man. Had they snuck around to the front and were waiting for me?

The guy was still on the ground, coughing.

As the dust cleared, I was not so happy to see who was sitting there. Troy. The chicken.

"What are you doing?" I asked.

"Me? What are you doing? You could have killed me, slamming into me that hard."

"Oh, sure, this is my fault. Listen, I don't have time to play this game. The Stooges are close behind," I said, running out of the tunnel and into the open air.

Troy was at my heels.

"I know where we can hide," he said.

"I don't need your help," I said, giving him the evil eye.

Then the hurried voices grew closer, and I panicked.

*Well, two are better than one.* "Where?" was all I asked.

I followed Troy into the gazebo, where he

wrenched open the top of the weathered bench seat and nodded for me to get inside. Our eyes met, and I had to decide in a fraction of a second whether I could trust him or not.

Deciding to take a chance on him, I jumped inside the bench seat and crouched down. For a moment, I thought Troy would shut me in, nail the lid down tight, as if in a prison cell. But he didn't. He squatted down in front of me and lowered the lid down, concealing us both inside the most uncomfortable hiding place ever.

Without further adieu, the Stooges descended upon the gazebo like performers entering the stage for a tap dance number. Their feet clanked on the wooden floorboards, even on top of the bench where we huddled. My breath was too freaked out to leave my lungs. I had to figure out how to breathe right.

A scratchy voice croaked out, "Where could they have gone so fast?"

"I don't know, but you know the rules," said a deep, serious voice.

*Oh, man. Which rules? There are so many stinking rules,* I thought.

The Stooge above us stomped his foot, the bench boards cracking a little beneath the force. I shut my eyes and sank lower, a snail retreating into its shell. Then he said, "Wasn't he supposed to help us?"

"Maybe he's on the wrong side after all," answered the croaky Stooge.

*Who's "he"? What are they talking about?* I wanted to look up at Troy, at least to see his expression but I didn't dare twitch a muscle.

Pacing back and forth above us, the Stooge said, "If he thinks he can hide out and make us do all the work, he is mistaken."

"Hide out . . . ," said the deep voice above. He seemed to be pondering something.

*This is it. He knows!* I thought. He had the same tone of voice my mother did when she would catch me daydreaming instead of organizing my sock drawer as I had been instructed.

*This is not good. What am I going to do? Maybe I could imagine them all trapped in ivy growing over the gazebo. Why can't I focus?* My mouth was so dry I couldn't produce a drop of saliva.

Then the deep voice took two steps closer to our bench and whispered, "I know where they are."

# CHAPTER SIXTEEN
# Oh, So Thirsty

My heart stopped beating for about five seconds. Just as it did when I first saw Aimee, but for really different reasons. I was ready for them to rip the lid off the bench and expose us, but they all just tromped away like a herd of cattle.

Troy and I waited a good amount of time before we cracked the lid and investigated our surroundings. With no Stooges far or near, we ventured toward the knotted olive tree.

*Whoo-hoo,* I sang silently as Troy and I sprinted toward Pierre-Louis's home. We ran along the backside of the estate property, hidden behind a covering of brittle shrubbery. We were taking the long way around, but I didn't care about a little more exercise. I felt relieved to be out of that cramped, *slightly* terrifying hiding space. Those dim-bulb Stooges didn't even think to look inside the bench in the gazebo.

Troy insisted he come with me to Pierre-Louis's home, just in case the Stooges were there. I didn't want him to come. The muscly chicken wasn't going to boss me around anymore. I had some ideas of my own. Plus, the words of the lion about "beware of false prophets who come disguised as harmless sheep but are really vicious wolves" was now the tune keeping cadence with my steps.

Upon arriving at Pierre-Louis's, we let ourselves in. I thought for sure Troy would stand out front as guard, but instead he came in with me. Pierre-Louis must have been in his room—the living area was quiet and still. The leftover buckets from my imagination planting service earlier were laying on their sides. But that was the only remarkable difference in the house, as far as I could tell.

While stacking the buckets in a neat tower, I remembered I was thirsty. The kind of thirst that can't be quenched with juice or milk or even bubbly soda pop—only water would do. I couldn't take this much longer.

Troy made himself at home, chowing down on a chunk of bread from the table. *How rude*, I thought. My frustration with this guy started to resurface.

"Why did you run away when we were in Snot-hook's lair?" I asked, wanting a straightforward response.

"It's simple," he said, crumbs falling from his stuffed mouth. "If we all got caught, there would be no hope for Fantaisie."

"You think you're the hope for these people?" I asked.

"They are my people, Walter. You mustn't forget. Plus, I'm the strongest. They need me," he said, very matter of fact.

I chose my words carefully. "So you would sacrifice Aimee, Crinkle, and me because without your big muscles the Fantaisies won't survive?" A hint of sarcasm may have slipped out.

Troy put the bread down and stood up. Uh-oh.

"Look, Walter, Snot-hook isn't going to hurt Aimee. They have history. Crinkle is incredibly resourceful, and he can handle himself. I thought for sure you would be right behind me. When I realized you weren't, I waited in the tunnel." He sat back down and propped his feet on the table.

*That must have been a long wait*, I thought. He sounded sincere, or maybe he was trying to be sincere. I couldn't quite decide.

The unbearable dryness in my mouth made me smack my lips together.

"What's the matter?" Troy asked. Clearly he was trying to change the subject.

"I'm just so thirsty," I replied.

"Here, have some water." He pulled a small canteen from his pocket and handed it to me. I unscrewed the cap and was about to take a swig when something stopped me. An odd feeling that sent tingles up my spine. I glanced at the container and then at Troy's gloved hands.

And I knew. *He's the crooked spy, not Crinkle.*

*I'm not that thirsty, dude.*

"Go ahead, take a drink, Walter. You look dehydrated."

*First of all, I'm not sure how someone looks dehydrated. Second, you're not about to poison me with Moxie water.* I realized that those bulging muscles weren't just for show. He was going to make me drink the water and drag me back to Snot-hook like the vicious wolf I now knew him to be.

"Yeah, know what . . . I'm okay after all," I said, setting the canteen on the table. We locked eyes, and I knew that he knew that I knew. A breathless, yet clarifying moment.

Just then, the door to Pierre-Louis's room swung open with a creak. Out walked Pierre-Louis with slightly rosy cheeks and a sparkle in his eyes. His cane was in one hand and his daisy in the other. He must have really liked flowers.

He beamed at me, but then his gaze fell upon Troy and his joy fizzled away like steam from hot soup on a cold day.

"You're not to be in here with your gloves on," Pierre-Louis said to Troy with renewed strength.

"Oh, come on. We won't be here long. And besides, I don't want to have to rush out and leave my gloves behind."

"Are you in a hurry?" Pierre-Louis asked.

"Well, you should be in a hurry," Troy retorted. "Walter here blew his top with Snot-hook, and now he has Crinkle and Aimee locked away in the gray room. They probably already drank the Moxie water." His words dripped with contempt.

How did he know I blew up at Snot-hook?

Pierre-Louis shifted and took a shallow breath at the thought of his children losing what was left of their imaginations. "Snot-hook has a ton of rules, but I only have one. Either the gloves come off, or you must leave."

I didn't recognize this Pierre-Louis, but I liked him. If a teeny daisy could affect him this much, somebody should give him a whole garden. Oh, I guess that someone was me.

Troy scowled. Silence settled over the whole land.

Okay, it was just extremely silent in the living room, but it felt like the whole world was waiting to see what Troy would do next.

Finally, he huffed, grabbed his bottle of dullness potion, and stormed out of the olive-tree cottage. I turned to capture Pierre-Louis's expression, but he was gone.

## CHAPTER SEVENTEEN

# Spunky Pierre-Louis

Alone for a moment, I consulted the lion. The paper lion was tattered from its adventurous ride inside my pocket. I pulled the tongue out and read:

*A fool gives full vent to his anger,*
*but a wise man keeps himself under control.*

*Oh, great. Now you tell me*, I thought.

"I could have used this bit of information a long time ago," I said aloud, holding the lion up to my face.

"Having a chat with the lion, are we?"

I about died—in part from the shock of his voice and partly from embarrassment.

Pierre-Louis had exited his room carrying a satchel

and his daisy—his newfound hope—tucked under his arm. He looked stronger, with determination etched in his brow.

Noticing my embarrassment, he said, "Oh, don't worry, Walter. If you find yourself talking to the lion, that means you're trying to understand."

"Yeah, I am. I'm trying to understand how I let Aimee and Crinkle get caught by that creep Snot-hook. I'm sorry."

Pierre-Louis shuffled toward the door. "We don't have time for unnecessary remorse, Walter. I'm feeling better, but I still can't move very fast."

*I can't let this happen again. I'm not going to follow blindly while other people play out their ideas on how to save this place.*

"Where are we going?" I asked.

"To a place we can speak in secret," he whispered.

"Okay, 'cause I have some ideas, and you said I was the savior and all."

"You are. However, if we don't get out of here, Troy and the rest of the Stooges will return, finding us twiddling our thumbs."

*Wow, this new Pierre-Louis is sassy. Now I understand where Aimee gets her cheekiness.*

I nodded and followed him out of his home and down a path. The sky dimmed as evening approached.

The path was as narrow as a snail's slime trail. Branches once again whacked me in the face and scratched my arms as I followed yet another Fantaisie through the brush. Every touch of foliage lit up with color and life.

Pierre-Louis stopped to take in the brilliant colors. In amazement he reached out to touch a spiral leaf. Then his soft eyes looked back at me and said, "Try not to touch anything, Walter, or you'll give us away."

You had to be kidding me. This must have been what they call déjà vu. Experiencing the same thing over and over again. I wasn't about to listen to an encore lecture.

"Look," I said, "I can't help it. Everything I touch comes to life."

Pierre-Louis didn't respond to my protest. He just kept walking. Soon we arrived at the base of a tree. We circled around to the back of it. Notches were etched out of the trunk. Place holders for feet and hands?

"Up you go," Pierre-Louis instructed.

"Are you crazy?" I whispered. "If I so much as touch this tree with my pinky toe, it will blossom and give us away instantly. Sir."

"Of course, but I've lined the notches with Crinkle's special fabric. So as long as you touch only the marked cut-outs, we should be fine."

"When did you do that?"

"Right after Aimee gave me the daisy. Crinkle had

left some of the fabric with me for safekeeping. I figured after you created all those plants for everyone, we might need a more secret place to hide. Now up you go."

Hesitantly, I reached for the first notch. Just before I rested my fingers in the groove, I closed my eyes. Silence from Pierre-Louis made me open my eyelids. He was right. Nothing happened to the tree. I just had to be careful. The tree trunk was particularly steep, and the shallow tree notches left me with little to wrap my grip around.

About halfway up, my foot slipped out of the protected groove and slid down the tree. Oh, no! Rich brown color filled the base of the trunk, moss clumped up and I swore I saw an ant climbing alongside me. I jerked my foot off the tree the second I regained my balance.

I glanced down below me to see a wide-eyed Pierre-Louis starting the climb himself. Grateful he didn't scold me for my mistake, I crawled over the edge into a tree house fort lined with Crinkle's fabric.

Once inside, I helped Pierre-Louis into the shelter. The cramped fort contained upside-down vegetable crates and a couple of buckets. It was much like the storage shed where we rolled out the map. The map that had the blue pickup truck, which reminded me of Uncle Andre and Aunt Cecelia.

*I wonder if Aunt Cecelia made the all-too-needed sale,* I thought. What if she had already come back to the truck and found me missing? I didn't think she could handle another missing person.

A gnawing urgency grabbed hold of me. I had to get back to the truck.

"Walter, what's the matter?" asked Pierre-Louis, staring at me from his apple crate chair.

"Uh, I have to get going," I said.

"We sure do. But you have to tell me those brilliant, lifesaving ideas first."

"No, I mean I have to get back to my aunt. She must be worried sick. I can't make her cry again," I said, slipping my foot over the edge, trying to find the first notch.

"I can't believe it," said Pierre-Louis as I continued to fumble around.

"What?" I asked looking up at him.

"In such a short time with the lion, you've already gained wisdom."

"The lion? The lion didn't tell me to go back to the truck and my aunt."

"What did it tell you?"

"It said . . ." I paused for a moment to think. "A fool gives full vent to his anger, but a wise man keeps himself under control." In that moment, realization filled the space between my ears. I pulled myself back into the fort. "I was angry and kicked the dashboard when I last saw her. I'd hate for that to be what she remembers about me. I should be waiting there for her with a cheerful look."

"I'm glad you have come to that understanding. And your aunt will be just fine."

"How do you know?"

"I just know," he said, tapping the top of a nearby bucket. "Walter, something important is unraveling here in Fantaisie."

I took a seat. His calm, confident tone had simmered down my urge to run.

"Walter, a garden has a life of its own . . . a heartbeat . . . and you have made ours beat again."

"What?" I gasped. My heart skipped and sputtered in my chest. "Uncle Andre used to say that," I stammered. Okay, I was freaking out. How did he know to say that? Why was the blue truck on their old map? Why did they recognize me. Who told him about the lion?

"Listen," I said, "I've been rather agreeable to this point, trying patiently to wait for explanations, but I'm done. I need to know exactly what's going on before I go or do anything else for you or any other elf." My hands started to shake, and for the first time on this adventure I was the one who felt like crying. "What do you know about my uncle Andre?" I asked.

Pierre-Louis looked deep into my eyes and said, "He was here."

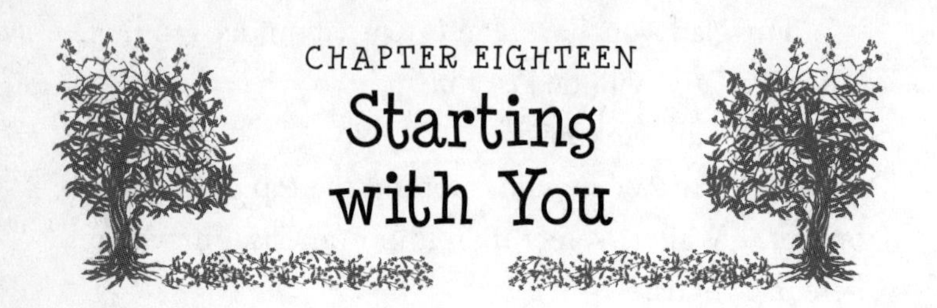

## CHAPTER EIGHTEEN
# Starting with You

Like a parrot on its perch, I paced back and forth in front of Pierre-Louis in the cramped space. I couldn't believe what I had just heard. Aunt Cecelia hadn't said she'd been here before. Although, today when we arrived she looked at the shabby house like she had seen it before. Maybe she had been here before. Until today, she and my uncle always traveled together. They must have been here together. I'd forgotten today was the first day she was selling all on her own.

"When was he here?" I asked.

"Oh, it's been several years ago now."

"Oh." I hung my head and sat back down on my apple crate.

"He was here long before Snot-hook started poisoning us with his monotonous rules," Pierre-Louis continued. "He said he would return someday."

"And he never did?"

"Not yet, I'm afraid." With a sudden realization, he asked, "Where is he now, Walter?"

"That's just it. That's the unexpected awful thing. We don't know where he is. He's been missing for three months." I could feel sadness swirling among anger bubbles, mixing up a sour concoction.

"I'm devastated to hear that. He was a lively, wise fellow. He had the Lifepower too, you know."

"He did?" I jerked in surprise and almost fell off my crate.

"Yes, except back then our garden was beautiful and his power only added brightness and extra color."

My mouth hung open. "I can't believe it!"

"So when you arrived, looking just like him and sprouting life, we thought for a moment he had returned to help us."

"Wow. I can't believe he didn't tell me. That makes for a cool story."

Pierre-Louis smiled. "I'm sure he would have told you eventually."

I shook my head. "You're right. I do look like him and somehow I have this 'power,' as you call it. But I'm not him, unfortunately. My uncle would have saved this place by now."

"Can't you see, Walter? We need you and your Life-power more than ever before. We need you now more than we needed your uncle."

That was hard to believe, but I shrugged and said, "I know. I just always wanted to come with him to a place like this, and now I'm finally here, and he's missing."

"But you are not alone," Pierre-Louis replied. "You have an ever-present guide, don't you?"

I looked at him with more confusion than I would have liked to admit. I should have known what he was talking about.

"The words of the lion." He uttered every syllable like he was talking to a kindergartner.

"Oh, of course. Yeah, the lion. I knew that," I said unconvincingly.

"The lion has helped you along your way?"

"Yeah, but sometimes too late and not always in the way I expect it to."

"So it's the lion's fault that you waited too long to consult his advice, only to then misinterpret the message?"

"Well . . . yeah . . . uh, I don't know." Why was I acting like such a baby? How could a piece of folded paper be responsible for my actions? My actions, my ideas.

"Hey, I have an idea I wanted to share. Something I think can really work in our fight against this crazy Snot-hook guy."

Leaning forward, elbows on knees, Pierre-Louis asked, "What is your plan, Walter?" He looked like he was about to unwrap his first and largest present on Christmas morning.

Hoping that what I was about to say was half as interesting as he expected, I said, "I've come to understand a few new things in my time here. First off, I've got to save you and the Fantaisies from this horrible life of boredom and despair and get back to my aunt . . . and then do the same for her."

I paused, uncertain if I should risk looking like a buffoon in front of this astute and sensible elf leader. Although, he did sass me several times on our way to the tree. Maybe he could handle a little . . . creative attitude.

Pierre-Louis raised a brow, "Go on, Walter."

"Okay, so, a cheerful look brings joy. What's cheerful to you?" I asked.

"Flowers. Brightly colored plants in nature," he said.

"Right, so my plan is to overwhelm Snot-hook's drabness with color."'

"All right, but haven't you been doing that already?" he said with cocked head and squinted eyes.

"No, I haven't. I've been hiding the Lifepower. It's the very thing that makes me your hero, and I've been stifling that joy. The lion also said, 'Discipline is wasted on fools.' Well, I'm not a fool and I have discipline. I will keep bringing the dead to life without stopping for anyone."

Pierre-Louis nodded in agreement, a huge smile stamped on his face. He kept nodding without a word, so I went on.

"We already know who the false prophets are: Troy, Snot-hook, Fantaisies with check marks." I could feel the tingling of a new type of bubble, one that would burst and spray joy all over everything. Excitement. "And I was thinking, since two are better than one, three must be better than two, and so on. We'll get other Fantaisies to change the dry land back to its glory with us. Starting with you."

Pierre-Louis's mouth shot open. "Me? How?"

"Let me try something." I took Pierre-Louis's hands, removed his gloves, and quickly examined for a check mark just to be safe. (All clear.) With his hands in mine, I closed my eyes and imagined him with the Lifepower, changing limp plants into full, blossoming ones, broken stones into whole blocks with multicolored patterns. Then slowly I let go.

Pierre-Louis stood frozen, staring at his hands. Perhaps he thought flowers might bud out of them or something. I gave him a little instruction. "Touch something. Try that large tree limb and imagine it beautiful and alive. Imagine the leaves, the way the bark feels against your skin with its earthy smell as it's warmed by the sun."

Pierre-Louis's eyes danced with joy. He stood and shuffled to the large branch that extended out from the fort. He laid his hand firmly on the branch and closed his eyes.

The air was thick with hope, and I once again found it difficult to breathe. Five billion seconds passed and nothing was happening. Okay, maybe only fifty seconds, but it was the longest almost-minute of my life.

*Oh, please work!* I thought. *I need help. I can't do this on my own.*

Suddenly, a sliver of moss crept out from beneath his hand, followed by the deep brown fuzzy bark.

I laughed out loud. "It's working!"

A mushroom popped out a few feet up the branch as the life weaved its way out onto the tips of the limbs where deep-green, needle-like leaves appeared.

Pierre-Louis opened his eyes, keeping his hand planted. He followed the path of his creation up the tree branch and absorbed the magnificent sight.

Then, to our surprise, a ray of light beamed onto the ends of the leaves and traveled down the trunk and rested on Pierre-Louis hands. Sunlight!

Through the branches I could see the sun peaking through the cloud cover.

*Sunlight, shadow. Sunlight, shadow.*

"I don't want to let go," Pierre-Louis whispered.

"I don't want you to either," I said, transfixed on the splendor, "but we have to see if the growth stays."

Pierre-Louis pulled his hand back one finger at a time, like he was playing the keys of a piano.

The new life stayed put!

A sly grin spread across my lips, and I turned to see Pierre-Louis with the same expression. *We can do this. We can conquer that drab, crusty Snot-hook!*

"What's next, Walter?" Pierre-Louis asked eagerly.

"Well, to start, I'm going to keep my anger under control and . . ." I reached in my pocket and found my dear friend, the lion. *I wonder what he has for us next*, I thought. Holding the lion up for Pierre-Louis to see, I unraveled his tongue.

I let Pierre-Louis do the honors. He read the words aloud, "As a face is reflected in water, so the heart reflects the real person."

"Uh, I don't know what that means. For our situation, anyway," I said.

"We'll have to wait and see," he said. "All in the lion's good timing."

"Okay, let's get out of here before the Stooges come for us."

"Agreed." Pierre-Louis stepped toward the ladder when a booming sound ripped through the silence.

*CROAK!*

Pierre-Louis and I jumped into an embrace. What was that?

My eyes darted around the fort. Pierre-Louis looked this way and that. Had we been discovered?

Then I saw it, nestled on the new large branch. We had been discovered—by a spotted green tree frog. It blinked three times, then croaked again.

We jumped again, this time letting go of one another.

I gave Pierre-Louis a manly nod and brushed off my hands like I had just taken out the trash. He cleared his throat and put his hands on his hips.

"Well, we better get going," he said and scurried to the ladder.

"Uh, yeah." I was right behind him.

Just as I slipped my foot over the edge, another *CROAK!*

I jumped a third time. "Okay, just stop it," I said to the frog.

How embarrassing.

CHAPTER NINETEEN

# On Y Va!

We were gathered with all the elves behind a stone garden wall. I showed the elves how to create plant life the same way I had shown Pierre-Louis. They were practicing on all sorts of things.

"Look what I made!" said the elderly bean sprout elf, holding up her newly created plant.

"Another bean sprout plant . . . great. I think we're going for more majestic plant life, but that's good practice," I told her.

"Listen, young man," she snapped back. "If you want my help, you're going to get some vegetable gardens—including bean sprouts and rutabaga, because they are my favorites."

"All right, all right," I said as I made my way

around the hideout. I was amazed at how many places the Fantaisie elves had created to store what was left of their plant life and unapproved trinkets. A stack of poetry books, a satchel full of brightly colored fabric, a box of paints and art supplies. The plants I had brought to life for them were lined up along the ground, with each Fantaisie adding to the collection with their newly given Lifepower.

"Oh!" cried a squeaky voice.

I spun around to see a startled little Fantaisie holding her bucket at arm's length. A caterpillar was climbing up the shoot of her purple flower and was waving around as if it were trying to tell her something important.

"Don't let little things like a caterpillar scare you," I said. "The more we bring the plants back to life, the more other life is sure to follow."

"Ha! When we were in the tree, you jumped like a scaredy-cat when that frog croaked," Pierre-Louis piped in.

I gave him a sideways glance, not bothering to mention he too had been as scared as a turkey on Thanksgiving.

Fears aside, I was confident that together we could overcome the dryness in the land. Now was the time to teach them how to use their imaginations to keep the Stooges at bay.

"Okay, listen everyone. Those stupefied Stooges are bound to come after us. So we have to be prepared."

"Oh no. What do we do?" asked the sweet little elf who had made the purple flower.

"Well, you have the Lifepower I imagined you to have," I said, "so you can use it to protect yourselves. Watch this."

A surprisingly plump little elf stood by the wall, munching on a handful of bean sprouts. Without him realizing it, vines were growing out of the ground and wrapping themselves around his ankles. When he reached for another handful of grub, he lost his balance, toppling into the dirt.

"Cool!" gasped an enthusiastic elf.

"Can I try?" asked another elf with his eyes closed, ready for action.

The plump and now dirty elf darted an unappreciative glare in my direction.

Just then, a Fantaisie rushed into the hideout. He was short of breath and trying desperately to formulate words. He propped himself against the wall.

"Are you all right? What is it?" asked a young lady elf.

"Wait," Pierre-Louis and I said in unison. He was still wearing his gloves.

"Take your gloves off first," I commanded. There

was no telling when another Fantaisie might cross over to the drab side.

Wrenching his gloves off as quickly as he could, he exclaimed, "Crinkle hasn't returned from Snot-hook's lair yet! He was supposed to meet me in his lab an hour ago. He must have been caught and thrown into the gray room."

Crinkle was going to have his brain freeze-dried. We were taking way too long.

"We've got to go!" I said. "Is everyone ready?"

Slack jaws, blank stares and rapid blinks were the responses to my question.

*Okay, they don't feel ready, but we have to start.*

"Ready or not, here we come," I cheered. That was all I could think to say. A saying from games of hide-and-seek in the backyard with Uncle Andre. He always knew where to find me. I was never any good at hiding.

And the moment we set foot outside these walls to light up this world with color, there would be no place to hide.

Dozens of Fantaisies without gloves gathered outside the stone wall. Mounds of various shades of green grass protruded beneath their feet.

This was so cool!

I stood up on a large rock and instructed, "Here's the plan. It's time to play!" For once in my life, I had permission to run, play, and let loose all of my imagination. I was in heaven. "We will start right here. We will touch everything in our paths, imagining beautiful, bright colors and tall, lush plant life."

"What happens when we get to Snot-hook's?" asked a Fantaisie with a scrunched-up, skeptical face.

"We'll create thick vines to climb over the stone wall and into his fortress. Once inside, you all will protect Pierre-Louis and me, so we can get to the fountains. But for now, just imagine this wonderful land of yours the way it used to be. Let's go!"

"Yes, *on y va*!" they shouted back.

Enthusiastic Fantaisies dispersed in all directions, eager to get their hands and feet on a dried-up fountain or brittle stem, or rest upon a rotten, broken-down tree and imagine it back to life. They left in their wake long stretches of green grass, rows of lavender bushes, and budding trees, as if we were in the peak of springtime. Clusters of grapes hung on limber vines. A gigantic sycamore tree re-birthed itself into smooth, curvy branches and wide leaves, like the ones on the front of syrup bottles.

*It's like a league of superheroes flying through the land*, I thought. I soared from plant to molehill. Wispy grasses jutted up through the ground, and deep yellow trumpet flowers scattered along vines, as if to announce our arrival.

All of a sudden, I heard a bird chirp overhead. Soaring over us, the blue bird landed in a hazelnut tree.

*Light. Color. Shadow. Light. Color.*

This was awesome! The plan was working. Wait, I hadn't been keeping a lookout for Stooges.

Immediately, I scanned the land. Was anything amiss? Sparkles of color caught my eye, drawing my attention to a sprawling rose garden. Then an apple orchard popped up, and even some bean sprouts came up. But where was Pierre-Louis?

I rushed through a bed of lilies shouting, "Pierre-Louis!" I shouted this way and that, but there was no reply. I ran atop a hill, scouring the land for any sign of my friend.

Wait a minute, at the far edge of the greenery, I saw . . . Oh no! Pierre-Louis was being dragged away by gloved Fantaisies, with Troy leading the way.

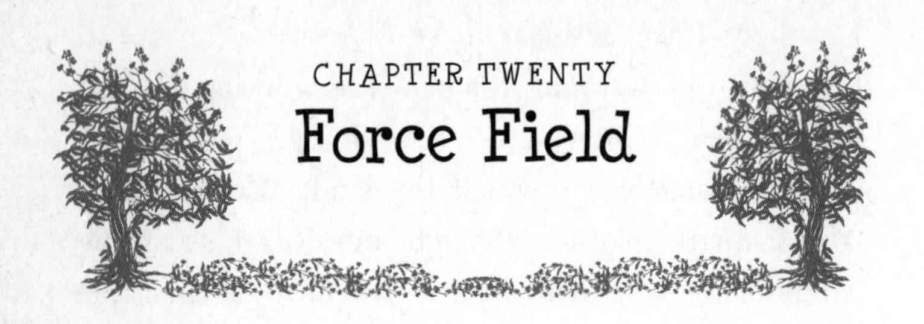

CHAPTER TWENTY

# Force Field

Several other elves also saw Pierre-Louis being pulled away.

"Walter, we'll go get him," one shouted.

"No, wait. They want to divide us. Let's stay together until we get inside. Once we're inside, we can rescue Pierre-Louis. Troy or Snot-hook won't be happy until they get us all. Let's not make it easy for them."

They nodded and went back to work creating the landscape.

We pressed on toward the gazebo without our trusted leader. Pierre-Louis's creative mind must have been too slow to defend himself against the drudge-like Stooges.

I couldn't lose Pierre-Louis. I'd grown to like the guy immensely. Okay, maybe it was more than that.

I looked up to him and I'd already lost my uncle, my best friend. I wasn't going to add to that list.

We neared the gazebo. The tunnel would most likely be guarded by Stooges. So we traveled around to the north, directly to the walled-off fountains. We would have to scale the rock wall in masses and ascend upon Snot-hook, like a drowning flood of imagination.

Just then, a gush of water seemed to come from nowhere, hitting and knocking a stunned Fantaisie to the ground. In the distance, a Stooge stood armed with a tubed water launcher. Streams of water propelled from his and several other Stooges' water launchers, instantly sucking the life and color out of whatever the water came in contact with. Bushes shriveled into dry, crusty mounds, and yellow patches sprinkled across the green grass.

"Oh no!" I cried. "Moxie water!"

The dazed and wet Fantaisie picked himself up off the ground and went back to creating new life, starting with the dry grass beneath his feet. His power was dulled and much slower as the Moxie water began to soak into his skin. The Moxie water was snuffing out the fire of creative life.

"Split up!" I yelled, gesturing for a group to go right, around the gazebo, and another to go left. The streams of water now shooting in different directions were unable to reach the other elves.

The drenched Fantaisie followed me around to the left.

"I think the water from the Fountain of Whimsey will preserve the new growth," I proclaimed while jogging toward the stone wall. My new buddy seemed queasy as he absorbed more and more of the water. "And it looks like you could use a swig of clean water yourself."

"Yes, please," he said. "By the way, I'm Alex."

"Let's get you to the Fountain of Whimsey, Alex. You're going to be okay."

We ducked and dodged sprays of water coming at us from random directions. Up ahead was Snothook's stone wall surrounded by Stooges with Moxie launchers.

*This is not good. What are we going to do?* Just as that thought danced across my mind, a group of Fantaisies encircled Alex and me like a force field, growing up large trees and hedges all around us. We should have done this sooner. Two are better than one.

The force field was thick with foliage and grew up underneath the Stooges sending them and their water launchers flying through the air. Now we had a smooth, undisturbed path to the wall.

Like synchronized swimmers, we stroked and splashed thick foliage and vines up the wall. The vines created a ladder, and we mounted the wall like a swarm of insects, not knowing exactly what to expect on the other side.

Just as we maneuvered over the top of the wall, a fire hose spray of water hit the first few Fantaisies, knocking them to the ground on the other side. They looked dazed but not badly injured. Good grief! Our shield of foliage had diminished with the climb. In a flash, the remaining vibrant Fantaisies cultivated another layer of protection with a miniature forest of pines.

Alex and I shimmied down rope vines along the inside wall. Once my feet were planted, I made a beeline to the Fountain of Whimsey, leaving poor Alex behind at the base of the wall. *I can get back to him once I get that fountain flowing*, I thought as I ran full speed. *As a face is reflected in water, so the heart reflects the real person.*

Snot-hook needed to see for himself who he had become. The Moxie water wouldn't show him the truth, but I had a feeling the Fountain of Whimsey would.

Two rather tough-looking Fantaisies flanked me like body guards protecting a pop star. They grew loads of irises and then ran through them, creating a pollen storm. Stooges fell to the left and right with sneezing fits.

The Fountain of Whimsey was left exposed, all the rocks still heaped next to the base, but without the dirt and weeds in between. In my last stride toward the edge of the fountain, I tripped on a root. I stumbled and toppled, and no matter how hard I tried to will my feet in front of me, I couldn't regain my balance. I fell onto the edge of the fountain and, to my surprise, the stone wobbled on its pedestal. *That's strange.* In a flash, I pulled myself up and flattened my hand against the still-empty basin.

"Please, work. Please, come to life," I muttered, imagining the fountain overflowing with clean, glassy water, enough to flood Snot-hook's whole sanctuary . . .

But I didn't feel anything.

It should have at least been getting damp by now. Maybe I had been hit by droplets of Moxie water during the fight to get here.

Just hold the image a moment longer.

Still nothing.

I opened my eyes and was horrified at the results. Nothing but dry, dusty stone.

*What on earth is going on? Don't panic.*

*Oh, that's okay, I don't mind having my brain sucked dry and spending the rest of eternity here in this wasteland without my Aunt Cecelia, crushing her heart a second time in just a matter of months.*

With those thoughts, I heard the most wicked laugh imaginable cut through the surrounding greenery, followed by ever-so-close, not nice footsteps.

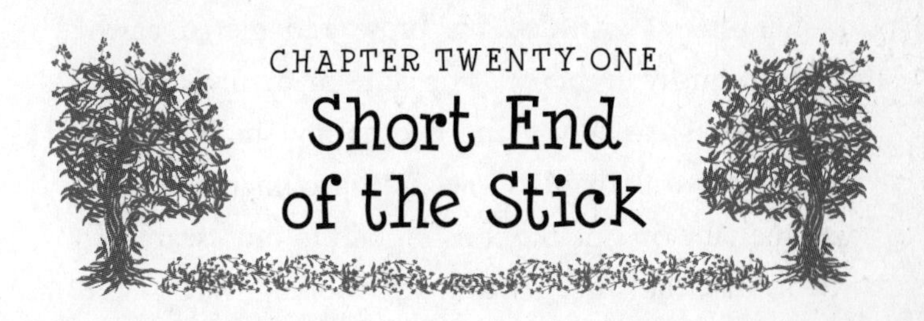

CHAPTER TWENTY-ONE

# Short End of the Stick

A sloshing wet Snot-hook sauntered toward the barren Fountain of Whimsey, followed by a string of ducklings—Aimee, Crinkle, Lucille, and Pierre-Louis.

I tried my best to appear nonchalant like I didn't have a care in the world. This empty fountain that's supposed to be full of lifesaving water is no big thing. I leaned on the edge and crossed my feet at the ankles.

Snot-hook stopped abruptly a few feet short of the fountain, his baby ducks running into his backside like a comedic stunt in a cartoon. The clumsy display kind of ruined his menacing entrance.

All of them, except Aimee, were dripping wet. I could only imagine they had been doused with Moxie water. Their eyes were dull and lifeless. Dehydrated windows to the soul.

Snot-hook wrinkled his brow and glared at me between bushy eyebrows. His stare made my stomach turn sour. I casually glanced over my shoulder with hope my two bodyguards would have imagined some jasmine vine or a prickly bush to aid in our escape. To my dismay, they too stood there, dripping wet.

Turning back to Snot-hook, I smiled, inhaled, and asked, "So what's up?" I ignored the surroundings of trees, some half alive, some in full pinecone bloom.

"You think you are so clever," Snot-hook said, sneering. "As fast as you create plants, I can prune them, if you will. A little splash of Moxie water, and your grand attempts to 'save' the land are foiled."

I felt a bit of Uncle Andre's bravery rise up within me. "I got it all under control." I had no idea what I was going to do next.

"Sure you do," he replied. "All you've succeeded in doing is helping me reunite with my favorite Fantaisies." He gestured to the lethargic group behind him.

Without thinking my question through, I asked, "Why is everyone but Aimee wet?"

Snot-hook laughed like a scary birthday clown. "I tried to have her tell you the story the last time you came for a visit, but she just couldn't get it out. She doesn't need Moxie water. Her shame is enough to keep her under control."

He looked at Aimee the way my father did just before he made me confess my latest rule breaking. He placed his hand on her back and she trembled. Pushing her forward, he said, "Go ahead."

She stood in front of me, every muscle and limb sinking as if she were a limp spaghetti noodle about to face a dousing of sauce.

"Aimee, what is it? You can tell me," I said. If Snot-hook was going to torment her, I should be the one to encourage her.

She raised cloudy eyes and said, "I did this."

I cocked my head like a confused puppy dog. "I beg your pardon?"

She took a deep breath. "I'm the one who asked Snot-hook to drink from the Fountain of Moxie."

That breathing problem of mine reunited itself with my lungs. Gasping for air, I eventually asked, "Why would you do that?"

"Because my father did not approve of our relationship and he wasn't going to allow us to be married," she replied, shuffling her feet. "I thought if Ickabod were more than just a handsome face, if the fountain could give him some wisdom, my father would accept him."

*Snot-hook got the short end of that stick—he's neither handsome nor intelligent*, I thought.

Aimee continued, "So I suggested to Ickabod that we come to the fountain and take a tiny sip of Moxie water, just to see what would happen." She started shaking her head back and forth.

"All right, that's enough!" Snot-hook interrupted. "So you see, you little amateur magician. Your sweet Aimee is to blame. Not me. She opened my eyes to the beauty of order and justice."

When he said that, Aimee's brow furrowed and a familiar look returned to her eyes. Would she punch Snot-hook the way she punched me? I could only hope.

Snot-hook didn't seem to notice. He spouted his speech as if behind a make-believe podium.

"Our lands are better this way with me in charge, instead of this nincompoop," he said, gesturing toward Pierre-Louis.

Aimee locked eyes with me. Something was brewing inside that pretty head. She ever so slightly nodded toward the empty Fountain of Whimsey I was still leaning against.

*What? I can't get the water to come*, I thought.

Then Snot-hook in his boldness jeered at Pierre-Louis. "It's also your fault, isn't it? If you had just liked me for who I was, none of this would have happened."

In that moment I realized that I couldn't make the Fountain of Whimsey work. But maybe Aimee could. Maybe, because she started this madness, she was the one who had to end it. I nodded at her to come toward the fountain. She looked confused.

Snot-hook's attention was still on Pierre-Louis. Up in his face, Snot-hook mocked, "How do you like me now, Pops?"

Ignoring Snot-hook, I attempted my form of sign language with my hands and facial expressions. I flashed a pointed finger in Aimee's direction followed by a nod to the fountain all with raised eyebrows. She didn't get it.

"And then there's this pathetic love story," Snot-hook said, circling around Pierre-Louis toward Crinkle and Lucille. "Crinkle. What a sorry excuse for a would-be brother-in-law."

I tried again. I pointed my finger at Aimee and then at the fountain. I laid my hand flat as if on the bottom of the fountain and then nodded up and down.

She started nodding too. I think she got it! Thank goodness, because when Aunt Cecelia, Uncle Andre, and I played charades, they could never guess what I was trying to demonstrate.

I was about to sign a plan, but before I had a chance, Aimee lunged toward the fountain.

She grabbed my hand, placing it on the bottom of the fountain with her hand on top.

*That's not what I had in mind!*

Instantly, Snot-hook spun around. Upon his command, the Stooges raised their water launchers and fired.

The Moxie water rained down just as the Whimsey water rose up.

*Two are better than one!*

CHAPTER TWENTY-TWO

# A True Reflection

The Whimsey water rose up over our hands, our arms, and flooded up to our shoulders. Aimee leaned in and took a gulp. I followed suit, and it was the most refreshing, hydrating drink of water I had ever had in my whole life. That lingering thirst vanished with only one swig. And the Moxie water sprinkling down upon our faces didn't harm us at all.

Suddenly, I felt cold fingers claw into my shoulder and yank me back. Snot-hook wrenched Aimee and me away from the fountain. He was yelling. No particular words, more a roar of sorts. Everyone backed away, starting with the Stooges.

Aimee hugged herself for protection as Snot-hook flailed his arms at us. Then he froze, a startled hamster, wide-eyed and skittish. In his fury, he must have caught a glimpse of his reflection in the Whimsey water.

The words of the lion immediately came to mind: "As a face is reflected in water, so the heart reflects the real person." *He sees his true reflection*, I thought. *I'd be freaked out too, if I were him.*

After a few moments, Crinkle, Lucille, and Pierre-Louis, still dazed, paraded closer to the edge to see what Snot-hook saw. Aimee and I took a few steps closer. Even the Stooges crept nearer to take a look.

At the sight of his reflection, a few gasped, Aimee sighed, and I whispered, "Wow."

Reflected in the fountain was the aged, decaying face we all had come to know. Not the young, kind of good-looking guy Snot-hook was used to seeing when peering into the Fountain of Moxie.

"No, no, no!" Snot-hook bellowed. He was about to splash away the reflection, but then he stopped, arm still raised like he was about to swat a pesky fly.

He took a step back. "What is going on?" he asked, shaking his head back and forth. He was frantic and twitching slightly. "This can't be," he insisted. "You're playing a trick on me with your imaginations."

"No, that's not true. You are finally seeing what we have seen this whole time. Who you really are," Aimee answered.

Snot-hook backed away from the fountain as if he had just come face-to-face with a skunk in an alleyway.

Maybe I should splash him with the Whimsey water before he gets too far away, I thought. But Aimee had another idea.

"Ickabod, wait. If you drink from this fountain, maybe you will be made new. Just like the plant life, you will go back to your handsome, young self. Isn't that what you really want?"

To my surprise, he didn't hesitate for a millisecond. He ran toward the fountain, cupped his hands, and took a swig, water dripping down his chin.

Then we waited.

One one-thousand, two one-thousand, three one-thousand . . .

Nothing happened.

*Not again! Why doesn't anything work like it's supposed to? Like we expect it to?*

Next, a Stooge, still equipped with his water launcher, stepped up to the fountain. He took a guzzle from the Fountain of Whimsey. In a heartbeat, light flooded his eyes, and he smiled.

Dropping his weapon, the next Stooge rushed forward and drank from the fountain. Soon, they were helping Pierre-Louis drink from the water with cupped hands.

Snot-hook just watched for a time, stupefied. I felt sorry for the guy. He realized he was old and ugly and apparently alone. Then, all of the sudden, he snapped to his wits and drew his check mark in the air, over and over again. Yet no one came to his aid.

"Why does it work for these guys and not Snot-hook?" I asked Aimee.

Frowning, Aimee replied, "I think he has to want to change. He has to want to turn from his evil, drab ways."

"Turn from his ways," I reflected. "That's it! He has to drink from the Fountain of Topsy-Turvy, the third fountain, because he was the one who made all these Fantaisies turn to his ways."

"Walter, you may be right. I never considered the third fountain. It's worth a try," Aimee said as she approached the frenzied Snot-hook.

Her bravery came with a huge helping of hope. "Ickabod, listen to me," she said. "You have to drink from the Fountain of Topsy-Turvy, turning away from your controlling ways. Only then can you be normal again."

Snot-hook backed away from her. "Why would I do anything you tell me to do? You're the reason I look the way I do. You told me to drink from the Fountain of Moxie! You did this!"

There were entirely too many *yous* in that statement.

"Please, Ickabod. I know I led you astray with that one sip, but I'm certain drinking from the Fountain of Topsy-Turvy will set you free." As Aimee continued to plead with Snot-hook, Lucille and Crinkle took their turns at the Fountain of Whimsey. Refreshed and clear-headed, they remained circled around the fountain. Their eyes were full of light, and peace shined from their beings.

"Look what you've done," Snot-hook barked, pointing at the glowing Fantaisies.

Aimee stood still, just shaking her head. "After seeing all this, you still want your dark, dingy rules to snuff out our creative light?"

A shadow of shame passed over Snot-hook's face. His chest rose and fell with heavy breaths. Tears formed on the ridges of his eyelids. He appeared angry and broken at the same time. He soaked in his surroundings. The chaos of two worlds colliding—groupings of vibrant pine trees, paralleled with dead, weeping ones. Patches of greenery clung to brittle clumps of twigs. Half gleaming life, half broken-down rubble.

Light, dark. Sunlight, shadow.

Then Snot-hook peered into Aimee's eyes and said, "I'm sorry."

Aimee inhaled deeply and smiled softly. "Just take

a drink," she said, taking him by the hand and leading him to the side of the Fountain of Topsy-Turvy.

Snot-hook looked inside at the transparent, potentially life-giving water. All was still and silent as he made his choice. He slowly pulled his hand from Aimee's, but instead of scooping up the water to drink, he said, "I'm sorry. I don't deserve to have my youth back, my joyful life back. My outside matches what I am on the inside."

With that he made one final check mark in the air and escaped down the tunnel that led outside his lair.

Aimee's mouth hung open, likely in shock. The last attempt to save her love failed.

Just then, Stooges swarmed upon us from all directions—over the walls on the vines and up through the tunnel. Backstabbing Troy led a monotonous march from the passageway, water cannons at the ready.

*Oh, great. We try to help a guy and this is what we get in return.*

With both hands, I leaned against the Fountain of Whimsey, and once again it shifted beneath my weight. Ducking down, I examined the base of the fountain, and then I saw it. To my surprise and delight, there wedged between the ground and fountain basin, was the most glorious kicking rock I had ever laid eyes on. The smooth rock practically glowed like the answer to a prayer.

"Crinkle, give me a hand," I said.

He rushed over and lifted the basin.

I yanked that rock out from under the fountain.

Then Crinkle let go . . .

The basin toppled over and water gushed out of the stone. Like a burst dam, the fountain flash-flooded the entire room with Whimsey water!

Whoa! That was more water than I expected.

The water knocked Troy off his feet. He floundered and splashed in the water, trying to get up but he couldn't find his feet. He eventually gave way to the flow of the water and drifted out of sight down the passageway.

The rest of the Stooges were drenched in life-water, overpowering their urge to shoot.

Water levels rose higher and higher, lifting us off our feet. We doggy-paddled to stay afloat. Some former Stooges relaxed into back floats as the water carried us all up and over the stone walls. On the other side, the water pushed us down the vines. Best water slide ever! Super refreshing fun!

As the Whimsey water spread over the land, absorbing into every crack and crevice, the entire garden sprang to life. Towering cypress trees, Christmas tree pines, and flowers and bushes of all the colors of the rainbow. Birds chirped and the clouds broke open and sunlight from the west cascaded over trees, plants, Fantaisies, and me.

*Sunlight, light. Yellow, orange. Sunlight, light. Blue, pink.*

*This is the coolest thing that has ever happened to me,* I thought.

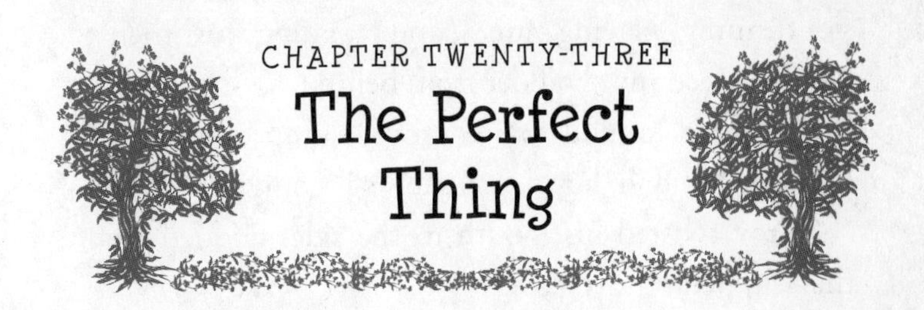

# CHAPTER TWENTY-THREE
# The Perfect Thing

I soaked up the sun, bright colors, and the now-fresh air.

Alex ran up to me. "Thanks, Walter," he said as he licked the water off his fingers as if it was frosting.

"Alex, you're better."

"That's right. As soon as that water flowed toward me, I gulped it up."

"Cool, dude," I said with a toothy grin.

"Fantaisies are drinking up the Whimsey water all over the place. We've started making piles of gloves. There doesn't seem to be a Stooge left. Thanks, Walter." He then ran through the garden, yelling, "Whoo-hoo!"

I shook my head and laughed.

The setting sun splashed even more shades of color across the entire garden estate. I imagined the Fantaisies running, playing games, and laughing. Just then a hand slapped my shoulder from behind.

I turned around to see Troy. I jumped back and stammered, "Uh, hey . . . so, how's it going?"

Troy twisted his mouth to the side, nodded, and then slipped off his gloves.

"No more check mark," he said.

Thank goodness. I just nodded back.

"Walter, I'm sorry," he said, looking me straight in the eyes. "You see, I looked up to Ickabod all my life like an older brother. But he never gave me much thought. And when he gained power, I saw that as my chance to get close to him. To learn from him."

His eyes glanced down at the floor for a second. Then he took a breath and lifted his eyes to mine again. "I thought if I could capture you, without anyone's help, he would respect me. I was wrong."

I placed my hands on my hips and tried to flex my arms. Troy's biceps seemed bigger then ever.

"Hey, it's cool. We're all okay now," I replied.

"Yeah. Truth is Snot-hook wanted to freeze-dry Pierre-Louis even more then he wanted you. He couldn't forgive Pierre-Louis for saying no to his relationship with Aimee."

"Well, sure, but I played a pretty important part in all this," I said, puffing out my chest.

"Sure, but I could have handed you over to Snothook easily." He smiled. That buff guy had the nerve to smile at me.

"Oh, really? Well . . ."

A double get-your-attention cough stopped our bickering.

Crinkle and Lucille walked up, arm in arm. They beamed with joy, swaying back and forth to the music of a blue jay. Then Crinkle said, "You're awesome, man!" and he gave me a huge bear hug.

Once Crinkle released his grip on me, he turned to Troy.

"I'll talk with my father. If you keep the gloves off, forever, he might let you be a Fantaisie again."

"I think I just might." We all turned as Pierre-Louis approached us and patted Troy on the shoulder. Troy bowed and stepped back to make room for the rightful leader.

Pierre-Louis's misty eyes rested on me with an approving smile. He offered his hand, which I shook firmly. "Thank you, Walter. Your uncle would be proud."

Instantly, I snapped back to my reality. I had to get back to Aunt Cecelia.

"Yeah, I think he would be. Maybe he is proud right now. I kinda feel like he was with me this whole time—in spirit, anyway," I said.

"Perhaps he was guiding you through the word of the lion," Pierre-Louis said.

"Perhaps," I responded. The urgency to get back to Aunt Cecelia grew inside me. Kinda like the itching curiosity. "I need to get back to my aunt," I said, moving toward the chateau.

"I'll take you," said a lovely voice.

Aimee appeared sheepishly from behind a pine tree. She nodded at her father, and we were off.

We walked single-file in silence through what was now a masterpiece garden, lush and fragrant. Cool green grass squishing beneath our feet. I readied myself for a backlash of branches in my face, but none came.

Okay, so I liked the girl. And I would miss her. I was gonna miss everyone. They kinda grew on me. I smiled at my clever joke, just as the chateau's roofline came into view.

Aimee halted just behind the hedge that had grown up under my bum.

"This is where we part," she said. She hung her head and scuffed at the new grass with her shoe.

*Now is a good time to say something that she will remember forever*, I thought.

"So, uh . . . it's been fun. I mean, I'm glad you got to meet me . . . wait, reverse that."

Perfect.

She laughed. A hardy giggle at my expense. Some of the sadness fled from her eyes and was replaced with joy.

That was the perfect thing to say.

We just stood there, smiling for a moment as a soft breeze brushed our faces.

"Uh, listen," I said. "I didn't realize about Snot-hook—I mean Ickabod and . . . you."

"Yeah, well, that was a long time ago. I just wanted him to get better, really. To be a better elf."

"Oh, yeah. That makes sense. Too bad he didn't want to be better." Oh, smooth Walter.

She nodded and stared at the ground. "It is too bad."

I looked up into the trees for a nice long awkward pause.

Then Aimee smiled at me. "But it is all over now and we have you to thank. I don't know how we will ever repay you."

"This land in full bloom is all the payment I need. Uncle Andre would have loved to see this," I said.

She nodded again with a big smile.

This time, I stared at the ground and she looked

up into the trees. She sighed, and I twisted my foot in the grass.

"Oh, and I'm sorry about chucking the rock at your head earlier today."

"I knew that was you," I said with a squint.

She giggled, then took my hand and gave it a tender squeeze. "Good luck with your aunt."

"Yeah, thanks. Maybe she won't notice."

Just then, we heard a lady scream from the front of the house.

"Or maybe she will. I better go. Bye," I said.

"*Adieu*," Aimee said before leaning in, kissing my cheek, and disappearing into the foliage.

My heart stopped beating for what felt like an entire minute. Now that was something I would remember forever.

CHAPTER TWENTY-FOUR

# Immeasurably More

I ran like lightning to the truck, ripped open the passenger door, and hopped in. Aunt Cecelia and a woman (probably the owner of the house) were spinning in circles, taking in the glorious garden around them. I didn't think they saw or heard me get in the truck.

I kept my eyes lowered, pretending I hadn't even noticed what had happened to the yard. A long moment later, the driver's door creaked open, and Aunt Cecilia climbed into the truck.

I could feel her accusing eyes burning a hole in me.

"Walter, did you get out of the truck?"

"What? Me? Nooooo," I said, and then I slowly peered up at her, bracing myself for a scolding. Did she buy that?

To my surprise, she wore a gentle smile. A smile that made me want to confess.

"Yes, I got out of the truck," I said.

She looked me up and down with curiosity, catching site of the lion resting next to me on the truck seat.

"Where did you get that?" she asked, her eyes darting up at me with a speck of hope.

"It fell out of the glove compartment," I said flatly.

She scooped up the lion delicately and rubbed the paper tab between her fingers. "What did the lion tell you, Walter?"

Huh? She knew? "It said all sorts of things that helped me."

"And what does it say now?" Her eyes glistened and an even wider smile spread across her face. I didn't think to check the tab now that I was back in the truck.

"Shall we?" she asked.

I shook my head up and down vigorously. Of course I wanted to know, because every time I read a passage, I hoped that there would be another.

She stretched the lion's tongue out far and read it aloud.

*Now to him who is able to do immeasurably more than all we ask or imagine, according to the power that is at work within us.*

Then she began to laugh. Not the painful laugh when the sculptures broke, but a light laugh. The sadness fluttered from her eyes little by little, like leaves blowing away from a raked pile.

"This was your uncle's lion, Walter," she said as she looked out the windshield into the garden. She intently scanned the trees and hedges before she said, "Did you find him out there?"

I knew she wanted me to say yes and have him walk out of the bushes in front of her, like a superhero emerging from the smoke of an explosion. But I couldn't. "Not physically, no," I said. "But I have a feeling he's closer than we realize."

"Me too, Walter. Me too."

She started the engine, circled out of the driveway, and drove down the road.

I broke the silence with, "I take it she bought your angel sculptures?"

"She did. She said they would fit perfectly between her three fountains."

"You don't say." I sank into the cushioned seat and smiled to myself. Warrior angels keeping watch and standing guard. "So where to next?" I asked.

Aunt Cecelia tweaked her head to one side, a sly half-grin painted on her face.

That was all I needed. She didn't have to say another word.

# Discussion Questions

- What are some lessons Walter learned from the lion?
- What kept Snot-hook from seeing his true reflection?
- Which fountain would you drink from and why?
- How did Walter's outlook on life change by the end of the story?
- How does imagination give life?
- How can you use your imagination to help others?
- What cheerful or good news can you say to someone who is hurting?
- The lion said, "Two are better than one. If one falls down, his friend can help him up." Who has been there for you? Who can you help up?

# About the Author

REBECCA LYNN MORALES grew up in Northern California. She graduated college with a degree in theatre arts from California State University, Northridge. She now pens the theatrics in her mind to paper. Rebecca enjoys life in Southern California with her dreamy husband and spunky Jack Russell terrier, Carson. She gives glory to God for all that is good in her life.

SCAN TO VISIT

WWW.REBECCALYNNMORALES.COM

0 26575 17802 9